I hated lying, but I could never, through all eternity, tell anyone the unthinkable things that had happened to me. Nor even the good things. I thought about the running in front of the big truck again, maybe it *was* the only way out! I certainly didn't want to be sent back to Daddy.

I'd read about kids who had been abused by their parents and then had been sent back to them to have even more horrendous experiences.

Other books edited
by
BEATRICE SPARKS, PH.D.

Finding Katie

THE DIARY OF ANONYMOUS, A TEENAGER IN FOSTER CARE

Edited by

BEATRICE SPARKS, Ph.D.

AVON BOOKS
An Imprint of HarperCollins*Publishers*

Finding Katie
Copyright © 2005 by Beatrice M. Sparks
All rights reserved. Printed in the United States of America.
No part of this book may be used or reproduced
in any manner whatsoever without written permission
except in the case of brief quotations
embodied in critical articles and reviews.
For information address HarperCollins Children's Books,
a division of HarperCollins Publishers,
1350 Avenue of the Americas, New York, NY 10019.
www.harperteen.com

Library of Congress Catalog Card Number: 2004099838
ISBN-10: 0-06-050721-7 — ISBN-13: 978-0-06-050721-3

❖

First Avon edition, 2005

Katie was my most precious pupil.
Katie was my most precious friend.
Then Katie was lost.

Foreword

Each year, hundreds of children are taken from their homes because of abuse and put into foster homes, some of which are not much better than their old homes.

Other kids are sent back to their abusive homes even when they cry out for help.

Most molestations are sexual and are never talked about. Studies suggest that only about one percent of boys who are sexually abused ever report their problems. Many kids go through their lives thinking, "If I can't trust my mother, father, teacher, or friend, who can I trust?"

*SUMMARY OF THE
NATIONAL INCIDENCE STUDY
OF CHILD ABUSE AND NEGLECT
U.S. DEPARTMENT OF HEALTH
AND HUMAN SERVICES*

In the past six years, the number of reports regarding abused and neglected children has continued to grow. Sexual abuse has nearly doubled, and emotional abuse and neglect were more than two and a-half times their normal levels. The trafficking of child pornography through the mail and via the Internet continues to increase. The total number of children seriously injured and endangered quadrupled during this time.

- Girls were sexually abused more often than boys.
- Boys had a greater risk of emotional neglect and serious injury than girls.
- Most of the kids feel unimportant and lost!
- "Where can I go for help?" is an inner cry that is floating around the world.

Finding Katie

Friday, January 2

I heard Mama scream, and I jumped out of bed almost without waking up. As I tiptoed down the stairs, I could feel my heart beating so hard that it was almost like it was going to explode!

By the time I got to the bottom step, Mama was barely whimpering, and I could hear Daddy still pounding on her. Scared to death, I slowly cracked open Mama's bedroom door and peeked in. Mama was curled in a tight little ball, lying quietly on the floor. She looked like she was sleeping. A big wave of pain almost washed me away into nothingness. I wanted to dash in and help Mama, but I didn't dare because I knew only too well . . . what Daddy might do then.

Daddy gave Mama another hard smack and staggered in my direction. I scrambled down the last step, hid in a dark corner trying not to breathe, and stayed there until I heard him zooming down the driveway, smashing into our big metal security gate on the way out.

Almost blinded by tears and fear, I crept beside Mama and patted her cheek, below her swollen eye.

"It's okay, Mama," I whispered, "he's gone."

Mama whispered for me to go back to bed. I wanted to ask her about lots of things but I almost knew she wouldn't tell me.

Back in my room, I put my pillow over my head and tried to smother out her crying. It wasn't like any human sounds I'd ever heard before, more like animal sounds or scary movie evil wailings.

Feeling freezing cold to the marrow of my bones, I wondered what Daddy would do when he came back. Eventually he always came back.

Sometimes he was crying and repentant, bringing gifts and flowers and candy. But other times . . .

I feel like I'm lost! Lost in my own home! Lost in my own body! But mostly lost in my own mind. Will the real, true me ever be found?

When the blackness of night began turning into morning grayness, I heard Daddy's car coast slowly up the driveway.

Not knowing if he would be Dr. Jekyll or Mr. Hyde, I held my breath until . . . I guess I passed out or something. . . .

I felt like I had lain in my black, cold, never-never-land bed for forever.

I was awakened by Daddy's "nice" voice, calling me "lazy bones" and telling me that I'd miss my school bus if I didn't scurry along.

I couldn't believe I'd fallen asleep, and more than that, I couldn't believe what had happened. Had it really happened? Maybe it hadn't!

Daddy gave me a pat on the head, told me Mama was still asleep, and said I should get Cook to fix me some breakfast.

All the way to school, I sat on the back seat of the van and wondered: Had it really happened? I was almost sure it had! Why wouldn't Mama talk to me about Daddy and his changing personalities? Or was it me?

It was probably me.

When I got home from school, Mama was like a zombie. All the curtains were closed in her huge bedroom, and only one tiny lamp was turned on. It was almost totally dark even though the sun was shining outside. I felt shivers go up and down my back and wondered if we'd all gone insane!

Time Stopped

I've become more hopelessly scared and confused than I've ever been in my life! And the physical pain through my whole body is almost unbearable.

Had I been dreaming? I begged Mama to tell me, but her eyes were glassy. I could hear my teeth chattering. Maybe Mama wasn't Mama anymore. Maybe I wasn't me!

I was so full of questions that I was about to explode,

but I knew that whatever had taken over my Mama's body wouldn't give me any answers. She . . . it . . . never did.

For hours I must have sat stoically by Mama's bed. My mind racing from blank to horrible, unthinkable possibilities. Cook came and knocked at Mama's door, pleading for Mama to eat at least a little something. Mama told her to go away.

Late today, Daddy came home with a new fur coat for Mama, a leather jacket for me, and a huge box of See's candy. He acted as if last night had never happened.

I went to my room.

Eventually **Mama** dressed, and we sat down to dinner with candles burning and soft music playing in our huge dining room. It seats twenty-two people, and with just us sitting there it always feels empty. Daddy told us how much he loved us and what a happy family we were and how he would soon be starting the biggest and most sensational project in Hollywood. It sounded dazzling, but for some reason spooky.

In the middle of dinner Daddy's cell phone rang, and Mama and I both jumped up to turn off the music. He waved for us to go to the library.

In the library, even with a fire in the fireplace, Mom and I sat silent and frozen while our dinners got cold and our hearts got colder.

Eventually we heard Daddy walking down the hall toward us. He was laughing and joking on his cell phone about some business things, saying Mama couldn't accompany him to wherever tonight because "she wasn't feeling well." Then he walked past us and out the front door without even a good-bye.

I helped Mama to her room. She always tried to pretend she was a queen when she was around Daddy. I wanted to scream and jump up and down but I didn't dare . . . Mama might . . . who knew?

Thursday, January 8

Mama and Daddy were going to a big Hollywood party. She looked more beautiful than I'd ever seen her look before. Her skin was almost pure white and her dress was like flowing, shimmering silver. Daddy had bought a huge silver-and-pearl choker and earrings for her, and it looked like the only thing she lacked was a crown.

Mama had always been a little bit quiet, but now she looked ethereal, like she was too spiritual, or something, to belong on this earth.

Daddy couldn't get over how beautiful Mama looked, and he told her over and over that she would be the most gorgeous, envied woman there, desired by every man who saw her. That made him smile in the proud, contented way that always scared me.

Anyway, it was nice to see Daddy treating Mama like she was extra special instead of . . . Pictures in my mind of him punching her and kicking her wouldn't allow themselves to be erased. . . . It didn't happen often, and rarely did he hit her where the marks would show.

I wish I could stop thinking about it.

"Have a good time," I whispered to Mama, as she walked toward the front door. She smiled but I could see that the lights inside her were still turned off! I wondered how she could always turn them on around Daddy when he wanted her to.

In my bedroom, I prayed over and over, "Please God, please, please, please, don't let Daddy get mad at Mama for anything tonight. She's too fragile . . . too hurt . . . too . . . everything sad and bad."

I can't understand why God doesn't make Daddy stop hurting Mama. Why does he do that? I'd like to talk to one of the nuns at school about that and a bunch of other stuff, but nuns have never been married or anything, so how would they know?

3:43 a.m.

Daddy was laughing loudly as he opened the front door and he and Mama walked down the hall. He was telling her that every man at the party wanted to get their hands on her and . . . nasty stuff . . . I didn't want to hear! I was glad their (his and her) bedrooms were downstairs, and I closed my door, crunched up tightly in my bed, and put two pillows over my head.

Friday, January 9

At breakfast Daddy told Mama that he had to go out of town for a couple of weeks and that she should never go anywhere without me while he was gone, even to her favorite shops in Beverly Hills. He gripped her shoulders tightly. "Understand?" he said in a voice we both very deeply understood.

As he walked out the front door, he hugged and kissed Mama like she was the most important thing in his life, and he almost ignored me. She just stood there looking like a fake, beautiful mannequin. I felt like a blob of protoplasm.

It's a yucky day!

I hate the cold! I hate the rain! I hate my Catholic school! I hate California! I hate Beverly Hills! I hate my teachers! I hate my friends! What friends? I hate life! I wish I was dead. Ummmmmm . . . maybe somehow I can reverse back to my old fairytale days where everyone "lived happily ever after."

Daddy doesn't allow me to complain. It's all right for him to do and say and act any way he pleases, but for Mama and me, we have to be exactly what he wants us to be.

Daddy would have a fit if he knew I was going to skip ballet practice to go shopping—not because of spending money, but because I'm never supposed to skip anything he has decided I should do. He couldn't care less how much I spend as long as Mama and I both look like phony models or something. He even had my thighs liposuctioned for my fifteenth birthday. Some birthday present, huh?

Mama and I came home completely exhausted and with bags full of stuff we didn't really want. I wish we could talk.

10:37 P.M.

I wonder why Mama and I can't communicate. She was "Miss Teen" something or other when she was my age, but only she and Daddy talk about that, usually in low whispers. And he laughs a lot when they bring out the photos and films that she won for her state and when she was a Miss America runner-up. But they never ask me to join them.

Most of my life I feel like I'm a chair or something that doesn't have any real importance or meaning. That's dumb because I have everything I want, or *they* want: piano lessons, singing lessons, dancing lessons, massages with my Mama, facials, and crap . . . crap . . .

crap. . . . Still I feel like something important is missing in my life! It's like I'm empty, completely empty, while I'm still trying to stuff insignificant nothingness inside me somewhere!

Mama spends most of her time in bed, in her curtain-drawn room. Daddy doesn't want her to go in the sun. He likes her soft, milky-looking skin. He's always whispering how "it turns him on." He, on the other hand, goes to his tanning parlor regularly and to his gym and club and stuff. I hate to even think this, but I'm usually glad that he's rarely home. He always has business meetings or something and has a suite in a Beverly Hills Hotel where he stays half the time.

Tuesday, January 13

Today has been the most wonderful day of my life! Sister Mary took eight of us girls, who had won student awards, to the museum. Jennifer and I giggled at some of the paintings that looked like two-year-olds had done them. Then we told Sister Mary that we needed to go to the bathroom. She gave us her scary you're-going-straight-to-hell look and told us to meet the group in the lunchroom in about five minutes. Like two happy little unleashed puppies, Jennifer and I bolted down the stairs.

We passed the dinosaur room, and we were in awe. These things are really worth looking at! As we backed toward the wall so we could better see the whole width and depth of the monstrous creatures, we crunched into two guys about our age who were as fascinated as we were. Together we talked about living in that time. The four of us were alone in the room, and it was like we had known each other forever. For the longest time we didn't even exchange names, but when we finally did, we also made up names. I was Olga, Jennifer was Luella, Mark was Aaa and David was Anagoge.

When we finally looked at our watches, we knew Sister Mary would skin us alive. As we started to leave, David and Mark asked for our telephone numbers. Scared about what Daddy would do if a boy called me, I kiddingly asked Mark if he could talk like a girl. He said he could, and so did David. We all laughed then and Jennifer and I scrambled up the stairs as soon as we'd given them our phone numbers.

We were shaking when we got into the lunch room, scared that Sister Mary might have called our parents. Thank goodness she hadn't, though she did have an aide looking for us. Jennifer lied and told the group that we'd found a little girl, crying and lost, and we were so concerned about her that we forgot about our group until we had taken the child to her mother.

Sister Mary said she was proud of us and told us to eat fast so we wouldn't waste any more time. We did, and the rest of the day we giggled and quietly whispered about Mark and David and how Jennifer would have to do penitence for lying.

It's strange, but I feel like I've known Jennifer for forever, even though I'd barely said "hello" to her before.

Jennifer's parents are as over-protective as mine, and both of our hearts were beating in harmony as we wondered if either of the boys really would call.

At our private Catholic girls' school, boys were like unknown creatures and, as I thought about it, I was never without a chaperone. I was either on the school van or with Mrs. Jolettea, or Cook, or Mama, or some other adult. Actually, when I thought about it, I couldn't ever remember being alone with any boy, even at birthday parties at Daddy's friends'. I always had people watching over me.

11:50 P.M.

I went to sleep crying again, dreaming that I was a princess locked up in a castle so big that it poked up through the sky. Still I was a prisoner, always tethered to a warden! Would I ever be released? Would I ever have someone to talk to who really wanted to talk to me and be my friend? Did my Mama and Daddy really love me? They never hugged or kissed me except when they were showing off to their friends. I wanted them to be like parents in old movies who hugged, kissed, teased, played games, and went to Disneyland, laughing and loving all the time. And never ever being hurtful or unkind!

• • •

When I woke up, I started to think about my childhood. I remembered once when I was little and I was sitting on Cook's lap in the kitchen. She was hugging me and singing to me, and I was purring through my whole body and feeling so warm and comforted that I never wanted to leave. Yet the minute I heard Daddy coming down the hall and calling my name, I jumped off Cook's lap and quietly answered him.

He screamed at Cook for letting me be in the kitchen and swatted me so hard across my bottom that I fell on the floor. Then he dragged me to Mama and told her what a bad child I was and how I was, even at my age, wanting to hang out with low-class people.

I was so little that I didn't even know what was happening. I just kept saying over and over again, "I'm sorry, I'm sorry, I'm sorry" as blinding tears cascaded down my face. It seemed they were both against me and there was *nobody* in the whole world on my side.

I wanted to go back to bed and completely forget about my parents. Instead I'd dream of Mark being my boyfriend and David being Jennifer's and the four of us running away together to a faraway, enchanted, loving land.

Wednesday, January 14
9:45 P.M.

Mark hasn't called so I guess he and David were just making fun of us. Or maybe David called Jennifer but Mark wasn't that interested in me.

I felt like the loneliest, most left-out person in the world. I decided to go out and swim a few laps in the pool just to get rid of some of the bottled-up sadness, or whatever it was eating me up inside.

Thursday, January 15

Today I met Jennifer in Sister Martha's class. Sister Martha is almost blind, so Jennifer and I passed notes back and forth. David hadn't called her, either, and we both said we didn't care because they were probably just a couple of losers, anyway. But we did care! I could see it in her eyes just like I could feel it in my hurting heart!

Blessed Friday, January 16

Mark called, and at first I really did think he was a girl! Mrs. Jolettea had answered the phone, and she said Sara Selznick was on the line. I was wondering who Sara Selznick was until I heard him laugh. Then all the sunshine of the world flooded in on me. "Hi, Sara," I said, and I didn't feel uncomfortable like I thought I would if he ever called.

I wanted like everything to ask him to come over and play tennis or swim or something, but I didn't want to be forward. Besides, Daddy probably wouldn't allow it. He loved having our house be like a convent except when *he* was having big, wild parties that sometimes rocked the rafters, while I was confined to my room.

Back to Mark. He asked me if I would like to come to his school dance in March, and my heart nearly leaped out of my mouth as I said, "I'd love to." Even as I said, "I'd love to" my mind was screaming that there was no way Daddy would let me go! He is from an old European background, which kept the family females in semibondage. Not really bondage, but certainly not the kind of free I'd like to be!

Mark and I talked for a long time. Mama and Daddy had gone out to dinner and a prescreening, so I felt safe. We talked about everything under the sun. He likes sports like I do, and music, and everything. I was amazed at how comfortable I felt on the phone with him. I wondered how comfortable I'd feel in person. And how I could ever, ever swing going to his dance.

I called Jennifer as soon as Mark hung up, and she

about broke my eardrum as she squealed that she and David had just hung up.

I envy her. Her parents are strict, but not as strict as mine. We've decided that we're both going to have to sneak out, and we can't imagine how in the world we're going to do it. We talked about what the nuns at our strict Catholic school (or our parents) would do to us if they found out. It could be house imprisonment for life, but we don't care. We're going to the dance anyway, one way or another!

Tuesday, January 27

Jennifer and I are being model students and human beings. We don't want to do one single thing that would annoy our teachers, parents, or schoolmates. In fact, for the past seven days we have been so hard working and sweet talking and pure and sanctifying that we're both afraid we're going to be translated and sucked up into heaven before we can even get to the dance. Fat chance!

Friday, January 30

We haven't yet quite figured out how exactly we're going to go to the dance, but we're so happy and positive and filled with joy and love for everyone and everything in the world that it's rubbing off even on our parents. I was actually talking to Mama for a few minutes before she went to her therapist, and when I asked her if Jennifer could come over and swim or play tennis for a while, she said, "Yes." At first I thought my ears were betraying me.

As soon as Mama was out the front door, I called Jennifer. Within thirty minutes Mrs. Jolettea was welcoming Jennifer and her mother. We talked for a while, then Jennifer's mother drove away and we went down to the pool house where we could talk about anything we wanted. We pretended that David and Mark were coming over in a while and we practiced our most graceful dives and most beautiful swimming strokes. We even decided we were going to teach ourselves a few water ballet routines to impress Mark and David if they ever can make it though our huge stone walls and iron gates.

Jennifer says her house isn't quite the stone fortress ours is, but it's still pretty much a prison in some ways. We've even wondered if we could burn candles and stuff to help us, or would that be sacrilegious? Just as we were getting deeply into the sacred; what we could do and what we couldn't do, Cook came out with snacks. I was really impressed and pretended that it happened often, which it never did. For a minute I wondered if pretending was a sin. I told Jennifer the truth instead and hoped I wasn't getting myself back on the road to hell. I don't need that now that things are going so well!

On the tennis court, Jennifer beat me to a pulp. It was humiliating. She and her brother played nearly every day while I had only my coach, who came to teach me for one hour once a week.

February, Monday 23

I'm trying to be more mature!

Last night I had a most fantastic dream. I was eating dinner on the patio overlooking the tennis court and I told Mama and Daddy how much I wanted to be a great tennis player but how impossible it was when I had no one to play with. Daddy, who is good enough to be professional, and often has professionals come over to play, said, "Hmmmm, that might be a good thing." I couldn't sleep for the rest of the night, I was so excited. What if he really would think it was a good thing! Jennifer could come over a couple of times a week to practice and . . . my heart was bubbling over with possibilities! Like Mark and David!

Tuesday, February 24

I waited until Daddy seemed to be in a pretty good mood and asked him about me becoming a really fine tennis player. I told him how much I loved to watch him play and envied his great abilities. That made him smile. And when I told him about Jennifer really squashing me, he said, "We can't have that." After I told him about Jennifer's dad owning three of the biggest hotels in the area and building others along the coast and that Jennifer went to my Catholic girls' school, he said I could start any time I wanted. I almost jumped out of my chair but that would not have been proper, so I just thanked him profusely and put my hand over my heart.

The minute I was excused from the table, I ran into my room to call Jennifer. She was as excited as I was, and we agreed that we would play tennis together on Wednesdays and Fridays if that was okay with our parents. We didn't dare say anything about David and Mark on the phone, but inside our heads they were rattling around.

Wednesday, February 25

Jennifer and I take the same school van, so I was just dropped off at her house after school. Like we promised our parents, we played hard tennis for an hour, then did schoolwork for an hour—and in between talked about how we were going to manage the David and Mark thing.

Friday, February 27

Jennifer came to my house and I honestly almost felt like I was in heaven with my beautiful, wonderful angel friend. She is the only really true friend I have ever had in my whole life. I had nannies when I was little, then when I started school (always private school) I had tutors; some of them nice and warm and friendly, others so strict and cold they often made me feel like a non-person and made me cry a lot.

Now I feel like I will never have to cry again! Not now that I have Jennifer for a friend! We did our tennis practicing and our lessons as we were supposed to do them and even found time for a little swimming and a lot of talking . . . mostly about David and Mark.

Mark is like a gift from heaven. Daddy is always gone on Mondays and Thursdays, usually all night, so Mark and I can talk for an hour twice a week. Last night he said that he felt he had known me forever and that he, who had never been really comfortable around a girl before, felt like we had been friends in a past life. He's told me everything about himself from the time he was little. His parents are Jewish and he has two brothers. His family travels every summer for a few weeks, and he's been almost everywhere in the world and seen almost everything. I envy him so-so-much! I guess because I've never been out of California. In fact, I've rarely been out of our estate, except to school things and stuff my parents consider educational. Oh, how I wish I could live Mark's life, with his teasing funny brothers and his loving mom and dad.

Mark said the day he saw me at the museum he thought I was the most beautiful girl he'd ever seen, that I took his breath away. He says all sorts of other wonderful, complimentary things. My parents have never been inclined to praise me in any way, so Mark's words were like sunshine and perfume floating into my life.

Mark is as excited as I am about our going to the dance . . . but I still haven't found any way to get out. Of course I haven't told him that! He's also asked if he could come over, but I've always pulled the old thing about my mama being ill and my feeling that I need to be with her since my daddy is gone a lot. Mama really is ill! She's getting thinner and whiter every day. Daddy thinks it makes her more beautiful and that her pale green eyes become larger and deeper and more "enticing" each day. He thinks she has a look like "no other woman in the world." It's scary to me that he's so arrogant about her looks and so almost completely uncaring about her health.

She used to stay in her room in bed a lot, but now she stays there most of the time! Actually, she doesn't even go to her doctor or her therapist anymore; they come to her. While shopping used to be her main hobby, now she doesn't care about it at all, which means I wouldn't ever be able to get out of my cage if I didn't have the Jennifer-release thing, and the too-wonderful-for-words Mark thing. Those two are my rock, my preservation.

Monday, March 1

Jennifer is coming over after school, so I pulled out my old blue bathing suit, which used to be my favorite. When I tried it on I popped out of it on top before I could even get into it! I had no idea my boobs had expanded so much. Well, I guess they should. I'll be sweet sixteen at the end of next month. Wouldn't it be wonderful if I could have a birthday party with all the fun and laughter that one reads about? That is so impossible it's not worth even thinking about.

Tuesday, March 2
4:23 P.M.

When I got home from school, Mrs. Jolettea was going shopping for some things for the house. She suggested I ask Mama if I could go along and help her since her husband was in the middle of fixing the clogged storm drain by the pool.

I begged Mama to get up and get dressed and come with us. Mrs. Jolettea could drop us off at one of Mama's favorite stores, or we could call a cab. She shook her head the slightest bit and whispered, "No thanks" as she turned over and closed her eyes. Then she surprised me by whispering, "You go with Mrs. Jolettea."

I worry about Mama a lot! And I wonder why the doctor and the therapist can't do anything to help her. But when Daddy comes, she perked up like a normal person . . . well, almost. I wondered if he was giving her drugs or something . . . then I hated myself for thinking that. What a suspicious rotten child I am! Daddy wouldn't . . . or would he?

When we got close to Rodeo Drive, I told Mrs. Jolettea about my being too big for my favorite old bathing suit. She laughed and said that would be number one on her priority list. I loved two-piece bathing suits, but I'd never had one. So I bought one one-piece and one two-piece. Maybe I'd never wear the two-piece in the pool, but I could strut in front of the full-walled mirror in my dressing room in it and pretend it was mine. I do a lot of pretending! I've done it all my life! Pretending is the only thing in my life that I can depend on.

Wednesday, March 3

Just before I left for school, Daddy walked in. He had an armful of the most beautiful, fragrant roses I have ever seen, and he invited me to come into

22

Mama's room to see what he had in the box. Mama sat up and ran her hands through her tousled blonde hair. In the soft sunlight that streamed through the tiny opening in the drapes, her green eyes looked even greener than ever, and larger than any eyes were ever meant to be.

Daddy opened the box and inside there was a flowing chiffon dress that was exactly the same shade of green as her eyes! Daddy and I both gasped.

8:06 P.M.

Miss Conders, Mama's dresser, came, and at 7:15 Mama walked down our staircase like a fantasy person, too beautiful to be real.

As soon as the chauffeur had driven toward the gate, I called Mark. He wasn't home so I called Jennifer. We talked until I heard her mother yelling at her to come downstairs and finish her homework. That was okay because I had my homework to do, and besides, I couldn't tell anybody anything about our strange home life, or was it strange? Maybe I was the strange one and everything and everybody else was normal.

After I talked to Jennifer, I tried on my two-piece pink bathing suit. I'd tried it on at the store but Mrs. Jolettea had been nagging at me to hurry so that she could get her shopping done. I really wasn't sure I could ever wear it in public, but I loved it! It made my boobs look like real boobs and my innie belly button look like it was begging for a piercing. But I'd never, ever dare do that!

I strutted in front of the walled mirror in my dressing room, and for the first time in my life, I actually thought I was pretty! The little white daisies around the edge of the suit made it look like a flower garden, and I wanted, for one time in my life, to show off!

I put on the pink rubber flip-flops that went with the suit and amazed myself even more. The big pink flower in the center of each flip-flop made me look like someone I'd never seen before! I knew I could never be as beautiful as Mama, but at least I wasn't the pukey pumpkin I'd always thought I was before. The pink in the bathing suit made my green eyes look almost as green as Mama's, and I took a deep breath and did the Mama stand. I hardly recognized myself. I was a young Mama, and I was amazed at what posture and confidence can do for a person!

Thursday, March 4

This has been a perfectly horrible, horrendous, embarrassing day. I finished my English paper and then left it on the hall table. Sister Mary chewed me out and made me feel incompetent and stupid. It wasn't like I did it on purpose! Then I caught my skirt in my locker and had to wear it all straggly for the rest of the day. Lucy Capputto called me Raggedy Ann. I hated it!

It's amazing how yesterday I felt so good and maybe even a kind of special me. Now I feel like crap again. Where has the pretty, confident, pink-bathing-suit me gone? Will she ever come back?

Jennifer and Mark both phoned tonight, but I couldn't take either of their calls because I was so depressed.

I tried to talk to Mama but she was out in fog land as usual.

I tried to talk to Mrs. Jolettea but she was too busy.

Daddy is out of town for a few days, but it doesn't matter because I never have been able to really talk to him!

So I talk to myself. Not very good company!

10:42 P.m.

Some kind of black explosive energy was growing inside me until I felt like I was going to pop and splatter all over my walls and ceiling. I wondered if I put on my magical pink two-piece bathing suit and flip-flops I could coax back a small, confident part of the yesterday me.

I decided it couldn't hurt or make things worse. As

I stood in front of my mirror and put on first the top and then the bottom. I truly did begin to feel different vibes! It was magic! And sure enough, as I looked in the mirror, I was smiling . . . both inside and outside! And standing and walking like the beauty queen winner! Not the runner-up!

Without even putting on a robe, I dashed downstairs and out the patio door, across the lawn and onto the diving board. Feeling like a beautiful flying bird I dove into the water. It felt cool and protective and I wanted to stay there forever.

Over and over I practiced each of my dives, my water ballet, and even a little dance routine on the edge of the pool. All the negativity and sadness in me was washed away! I'd once seen an old Esther Williams swimming movie and I felt like a young "her"; beautiful, talented, supremely happy, confident, and self-reliant.

When my head popped out of a complete underwater pool swim, I looked up to see Daddy's face staring down at me. I was so scared and frustrated that I started swallowing water and choking. Before I knew what was happening Daddy had jumped into the shallow end of the pool with his clothes on and was slapping me on the back, then carrying me up the steps, hugging me so hard I could barely breathe.

I was shaking with fear at the thought of what he would do to me when he placed me on a lounge then settled cross-legged on the tile floor beside me.

I was totally surprised when he tenderly picked up my hand, kissed it, and told me I was the most beautiful creature he had ever seen in his life, and that he had been standing at his window watching me from the minute I walked down the patio steps. Over and over he said wonderful, heartwarming things about me. Things I never thought he would.

It was strange because I'd always thought he didn't like me very much. After a few minutes he sloshed into the cabana to get me a huge warm towel. As he picked me up to wrap me in it, he held me tightly against his body. I pulled away but of course *that* was "my evil thought."

Sister Mary has told me a number of times that I'm full of evil thoughts.

Oh please, dear God, don't let me have evil thoughts about my dear daddy.

After a little more verbal soothing and him stroking my arms and hair, we walked into the house hand in hand, and he continued to say warm, special, loving things about me.

He says I am "the light of his life," that I always have been and always will be!

I went to go to sleep thinking Daddy loves me! Daddy loves me! Daddy loves me! What more could I possibly ask out of life?

Oh, and Daddy says he's going to start calling me Kathryn instead of Katie now that I'm a young adult.

He kissed me gently on the cheek and said, "Good night precious Kathryn, sleep well" before he left my room. My whole insides were about to burst.

I am filled from my feet to the tip of my head with joy and gratefulness!

Friday, March 5

Even Sister Mary noticed the change in my attitude; love and kindness and caring were flowing out of me like a "holy stream." I'm going to try, with all my heart, to keep my life like this, every minute of every single day as long as ever I shall live.

I truly believe now that Sister Mary is right, "As one loves others, they will love back." That was probably my problem with Daddy. I was afraid of him, so I couldn't love him. Now it's going to be like we totally understand each other.

Happiness is coming out of my ears!

9:30 P.M.

Mark called tonight, and it was like all the happiness and contentment in creation were mine. Only two more weeks and we will be together. It's kind of like a game with us counting each day till . . . UTOPIA! At first he couldn't understand why I couldn't meet him at the mall or something, but when he found out how super strict both Jennifer's and my folks are, he respected them and us, saying that at his school guys were sometimes vulgar and disrespectful of girls.

Then he softly said that I was the kind of girlfriend his mother had always talked about him waiting for, and that we had probably learned more about each other on the phone than we would have in person. At least he felt that way about it and I guess maybe I do, too, but maybe not!

I'd dearly love having him over here playing tennis with me and swimming and doing our homework together and stuff. But in a way it's true that just talking can bring out things that couldn't come out any other way. Mama and Daddy practically never talk to each other. Sometimes he talks *at* her but . . . I don't know what I'm talking about. I just know that all four of us, Jennifer, David, Mark, and I, are having a lot of fun with this silly little game we're playing. I often wonder what makes me think we can ever get together after the dance. But I can't let myself think about that. We will find a way!

Saturday, March 6

Daddy was waiting for me when I woke up and asked me if I'd like to play a little tennis with him. Would I like to? Do birds poop on your patio? I shouldn't have written that; it's low class and Daddy can't stand "low-class things."

1:30 P.M.

Daddy aced me the first few times. Then I knew I had to play my very best to impress him! I just about wore my heart out after that and he began shouting, "Good shot," until I finally got my confidence up to where I could play a pretty good game. I don't know when I've had more fun in my life, or more lovely feelings!

Daddy was going to take me to lunch at his club to "show me off," but some business person called and he said we'd have to do it another day. At first I felt so abandoned that I thought I was crumbling from the inside out. Then I remembered how much my Daddy now cares for me and how much I deeply and completely love and admire him!

Sunday, March 7

Yesterday afternoon, Daddy bought me an unbelievable white silk pants suit. When he saw me in it, he smacked his lips and said, "My baby is not a baby anymore." Then he gave me a big hug and kiss and danced me around the store. All the ladies who worked there were laughing and telling me what a wonderful father I had. I thanked them and blew kisses to them and him!

4:57 P.M.

Daddy took Mama and me to the Los Angeles Country Club for a late lunch, and for the first time in my life I created more attention than Mama. She looked beautiful in her soft lilac dress, but Daddy's male friends, who were buzzing around like bees, paid more attention to me than to her! Who would have believed it?

11:32 P.M.

After Mama had gone up to bed, Daddy and I sat out on the patio and talked about his new project. He was thrilled about it and excited that I was interested in his plans. After a while, he choked a little and told me how worried he was about Mama. I had been worried about her for a very, very long time, too, but hadn't known what to do about it.

Daddy pulled his chair closer to mine and held my hands. Then he told me we'd have to work together to help Mama. I felt tears running down my face as I assured him I'd do anything. He pulled his chair over closer to mine and hugged me and kissed me on the cheek. He explained that for many years, Mama had a problem with alcohol. While he tried to do everything he could, sometimes he simply lost control as he thought about me and how Mama was hurting my mental and physical and spiritual growth. He held me tightly then and asked me to please try to understand and forgive him. I hugged him back and thanked him for confiding in me. Suddenly he stood up and pulled me close, then almost violently pushed me away, saying he had to go somewhere for a couple of hours.

I wanted to beg him to stay with me and tell me more—about his work, and Mama's background, and everything else that I didn't know about. I know practically nothing about either one of them. It is like they had both just beamed down from foreign planets.

I tried to hug him again as he walked away but he pushed me back. "We'll talk tomorrow," he said in his strange, cold old-Daddy voice.

I plodded upstairs. All the warmth and brightness that had enveloped my new life with Daddy slowly leaked out of my body and brain. I was again my old lonely, un-belonging, hurting self.

What had I done to offend him? I would do anything to have him like me! Anything! Anything! Anything!

• • •

Never have I had such a comfortable, loving, belonging, experience in my life as I've had with Daddy the past few days. How could I have wrecked it? Will he now go back to being the old scary stranger who sometimes gets completely out of control?

I'm thoroughly confused. At one point, when Daddy and I were talking, we were so close and relaxed that I almost really did feel like I could ask him anything. Thank goodness I didn't because maybe . . . yeah . . . maybe the world is going to come to an end right here and now! I wish it would; this very second! And it would be over with!

1:30 a.m.

I cried in bed for a long time and waited for Daddy to come home so that I could beg his forgiveness for whatever it was that I had done to upset him. Then suddenly I thought about Mark and that maybe I won't always have to go to a Catholic girls' school! I certainly don't want to. Yet here I am.

Come on Self; think happy, happy, happy, Mark, Mark, Mark, dance, dance, dance! Who knows what wonderful happenings can pop up?

2:30 a.m.

Maybe I won't need Daddy's closeness. I'll always have Jennifer! Females are much more dependable than males . . . but then there is Mama. Is she the one who drives Daddy crazy?

Forget that! Move on!

Okay! When I go over to Jennifer's for our tennis lessons and to do our homework, her Mom is buzzing around like a little bee, and laughing and talking and scolding (but nicely) when we goof off. Her brother sometimes helps us with little things we could improve on in our tennis game, and sometimes Jennifer's mom and dad even join us in playing doubles. That is really super fun . . . and funny! It's like being in another land in another time and space, with another species of Homosapiens!

I wish my family was like that. But wishing means nothing; it never has! I should know, I've been wasting my breath on it all my life.

Wednesday, March 10

Today I was walking around the grounds trying to figure out how I was going to get out and back into my castle without a moat, for Mark's dance, and suddenly a miracle happened! Really! Plain as day I could see the emergency ladder that was under my bed in case of a fire or an earthquake or something. I could sling it over the fence by the pine trees, just like I'm supposed to sling it out of my window in case of a fire or something. Glory, glory hallelujah! I'm like Rapunzel! I can go to the dance! I swear to myself here and now that I will light a hundred candles at church. Well, maybe not a hundred but enough to show my appreciation for that absolute miracle!

There might be some minor obstacles, like maybe having to take my dress and shoes in a sack and climb over the fence in my underwear, but big deal. Only nine more days!

Jennifer is going to take the extra kitchen door key that hangs in their hall and sneak down the alley behind her house to the corner where she'll meet David. Then they'll come get me two houses to the right of my house.

When I close my eyes, I'm at the dance already. I wonder what kind of car Mark has? I hope it's not a convertible because I'm going to spend hours on my hair and make-up. I wish I could call Miss Conders, Mama's dresser, but of course that's out of the question!

Sister Mary got really upset with me today because I couldn't concentrate, but I can't! All I can think about is Mark and the dance . . . and all the other things I've never had a chance to experience. Will Mark really like me in person, or will he think I'm a total empty box? Which I probably am!

Thursday, March 11

Eight more days!

Sunday, March 14

Five days left. I am trying so hard to keep up with my schoolwork that my brain aches. I've got to keep up or get ahead, because if Sister Mary puts me in detention, I don't know what I'll do . . . or what Daddy will do. I don't want him to ever, ever, ever get mad at me or disgusted with me for being a dumb-head or anything else that isn't worthy of him. And he's always so busy, I don't want to upset him.

Monday, March 15

Four days left!

Sister Mary read my health essay to the class. I was a little embarrassed when she mentioned that I was the only student who combined mental health and physical health into the same category. To me, it's incomprehensible to think of good health in any other way.

That perked me up some, and now I feel pretty sure that I can make it till Friday—fantastic, fabulous Friday!

Tuesday, March 16

Three days!

I've tried on everything in my closet and nothing seems appropriate. Neither Jennifer nor I have the slightest idea what the other girls will be wearing. It's a private Jewish boys' school dance, so all the other girls who are invited will know the "rights and wrongs" and "dos and don'ts." While we will be just a couple of out-of-place dust bunnies.

Daddy drove in right after the school van dropped me off. I had my homework spread out on a patio table. I didn't want to do any work because the weather was so perfect. Both the pool and the tennis court were beckoning for me to please come down to them. I was trying to be strong when Daddy spotted me and ran up with a box of candy in one hand and a pink silk jacket and skirt, practically the identical shade of my pink bathing suit. He gave me the candy, skirt, and jacket then hugged me right off the floor.

"I've been thinking about you all day, baby," he said in a very serious way, "thinking about the days and weeks and years I've wasted trying to make money when I should have been here swimming with you and playing tennis and," he laughed, "going to Disneyland."

I started laughing, too, and he picked me up and started swinging me around.

After a minute or two he reached over, closed my books, and told me he'd send a note to Sister Mary excusing me from tomorrow's assignments. Then he swatted me playfully on the bottom and told me to go get my tennis things and bathing suit, he grinned, "The pink one that makes you look like the world's youngest bathing suit queen."

I blushed and he yelled "Last one in the pool is a rotten egg."

We swam and played waterball for a little while, then sat on the pool steps. He told me my whole life's story, from the first time I'd wrapped my teeny tiny baby fingers around his ring finger, till today. He was almost crying as he told me how sorry he was that he had missed so much of my life and begged me to let him catch up on what he'd missed.

After that we played tennis, and he taught me some of the tricks that his professional buddies had taught him, all the time treating me like a princess! I felt so beautiful and powerful and important that I wasn't even me anymore.

After that we drove to Santa Monica in his little black convertible Mercedes, which I'd never been in before. I told him how dreamy it was, and he laughed and said that if I was good to him he'd give me one for my sixteenth birthday.

He asked me where I wanted to eat and I said, "McDonald's," knowing that none of his friends would be there!

When we got home we sat in the car and Daddy told me he didn't want to tell me about Mama's problems, but he felt I should know. He sniffled a few times and wiped his nose on his silk handkerchief, then he grabbed my hands and held them so tightly they hurt.

After a few silent seconds he whispered, as though it was the hardest thing he ever had to say in his life, "From . . . from . . . from the moment you were born, your beautiful mama was so jealous of you . . . my heart began to break. Nurses and nannies were your mama, while your real mama devoted her life to being beautiful." He put his hands over his face and dropped his head. I moved over, hugged him, and lovingly stroked his face and arm, whimpering that I didn't know what a hurtful life he had been living and that now I understood why he had sometimes lost his temper.

We cried together like two little unloved orphans, and he told me how Mama was drinking even when she was pregnant with me and how it about drove him crazy. He said he did everything he could to get her to stop, but she either couldn't or wouldn't. Then a few years later she started using drugs. He put his head in my lap and I ran my fingers through his hair and kissed his face as he sobbed that the two of us would have to make it together.

"We can," I sobbed, and my heart thumped with a mixture of joy and sorrow that didn't make sense. I wanted to ask him what we were going to do about Mama, but of course it wasn't the time for that.

At my room Daddy hugged me and kissed my face and ears and hair like he never wanted to let go and I didn't want him to! We were making up for all the lost years that we had suffered through because of selfish, self-centered Mama!

Finally I pulled away and he sort of stumbled down the hall like an old beaten man. Poor, poor Daddy. What a sad, sad life he has lived with such a self-indulgent, egotistic wife who never thought of anyone but herself. My heart bled for him, and I hated myself for having thought all my life that he was the bad one.

I wanted to go into Daddy's room and comfort him, ask his forgiveness for all the bad thoughts I've had about him. He has been kind of like a stranger in my past, but now he is the kind of daddy ever child wanted and needed. I love him so much I can feel the admiring devotion coming out of my pores. I hope he can feel what I am feeling!

Wednesday, March 17
6:01 a.m.

I woke up and sat up in bed like I'd been shocked. I've been so busy thinking about Daddy that I had totally forgotten that in two days I will be going to Mark's dance! Or will I? Maybe now that Daddy and I were becoming so close . . . I feel absolutely physically torn. Can I possibly have them both? What a time for a situation like this! I can't wait to get to school so I can talk to Jennifer.

7:30 a.m.

I couldn't believe it when I walked past the dining room. The end of the huge table was set for two, with flowers and as much formality as there could be. I crept toward the kitchen where I always have breakfast, thinking Daddy must be having someone special from his company coming over.

As I hurried toward the end of the hall, Daddy bounced by. He picked me up and swung me around and around until I was dizzy. Then he formally took me into the dining room, telling me that he and I were going to have breakfast together every morning that he could make it!

Oh yes, and he wants to do everything in the world he can to make me happy and to make up for every second of our lost time! I am so excited I am about to burst!

But what if he wants to take me someplace special Friday night? Never have I felt so frustrated! Mark would never speak to me again . . . and Daddy . . . Oh, I'm going to miss my ride to school. Bye . . . everything in my life.

10:34 a.m.

Sister Mary thinks I'm writing down the answers to her dumb questions when actually I'm having a euphoric (I've always wanted to use that word) experience. Like I'm bubbling inside.

Today I was more than a little bit scared when I handed Sister Mary the note that Daddy had written, excusing me from my homework. I could feel my whole body shaking as she read it. When she had finished she flashed me a little smile and nodded her head. I about fell off my chair.

Daddy had told me that he had given my school so much money that no one there would dare not do whatever he asked. That made me feel important and confident. Like maybe, after all, I was somebody!

Thursday, March 18

Happy morning!

Daddy was in the driveway this morning waiting for me. He waved me into the car and said he would be taking me to and from school every day that he could, from now on. I reached over and spread kisses all over the side of his face. He laughed and said he wondered what Cook would think if she was peeking out the window. We both laughed at that!

Now the greatest thing in creation—Daddy said that he had to go to San Francisco for the weekend on business, and wives were invited, so he'd have to take Mama and her dresser. They would have to leave this afternoon. My whole insides fluttered. All my problems were answered! I, Cinderella, would get to go to the ball after all! Hurrah! Hurrah!

Mrs. Jolettea would be staying in our house, in the maid's room instead of in her apartment over the garage, while Mama and Daddy were gone. I'd tell her I was very tired so I'd go to bed extremely early and sleep in as late as I could. My insides were gleefully dancing even as I was lying! Imagine everything turning out absolutely like the fairy-tale way I always hoped it would. This couldn't possibly be all bad!

Friday, March 19—Mark!!!

I have fixed my hair a dozen different ways and used all of Mama's lotions and potions. I've tried on every dress and pair of shoes I own. Finally I decided on my green dress to go with my green eyes. I may not be anywhere near as beautiful and regal-looking as Mama, but I think I still look pretty good. I hope Mark will think so, too, and that I won't get all tongue-tied and brain-locked when I see him! I don't think I've ever felt so insecure in my life.

What a picture! Me climbing over our tall rock fence in my underwear and bare feet on the rope emergency fire ladder, probably messing up my hair and maybe having the ladder break, or fall, or some other silly thing that would embarrass me for life!

Oh, sweet Jesus, help me through this terrible dalliance! I shouldn't have written that! It's not my place to ask for help when I'm not sure at all that I'm doing the right thing, but I'm going to do it anyway. Maybe something awful will happen at the dance, but I won't allow myself to think about anything like that! I won't! I won't!

12:45 P.m.

I can't believe I'm not dreaming! Every single thing went so smoothly it was like it wasn't real. No one spied me when I ran, in my underwear and bare feet, to the wall, and I didn't snag my dress on any limbs as I put it on, and I wasn't accosted by all the bad guys in the world as I hurried past the Lavine and the Travolta estates.

Mark, David, and Jennifer were waiting for me by the Bells' and Mark, who was driving, got out and opened the door for me. He looked like Brad Pitt and I couldn't believe that he was as interested in me as I was in him. We laughed and joked about meeting at the museum with the dinosaurs and even called each other by our made-up names.

The dance was spectacular! And obviously it was a

rich boys' school. There were small tables with school- colored cloths that swept to the floor and a buffet that was furnished by Wolfgang Puck's. The band was fantastic, and while there were a lot of adults around, no one seemed to care.

During the evening they also had a couple of entertainers. A young girl and guy who were really funny, and a lady who told fortunes. She called up people from the group and told things about them that made everyone laugh and wonder if it was a set-up.

Anyway, there was not one single glitch in the whole evening. None of us wanted it to ever end. The guys let Jennifer out first and waited until they saw her walking up the back steps. Mark insisted on helping me get over the wall. He had no idea that it would have been easier for me to do it by myself in my underwear. As it was, I caught my skirt on a branch and practically fell over backward. Thank goodness he was there to catch me. He's asked me if we would be getting together again soon and, not being able to lie to him, I said, "I hope so." I really do hope so!

Mark tossed up his side of the ladder and whispered that he had never had a better time in his life. I felt tears run down my face as I whispered back that I felt the same way!

Saturday, March 20
6:25 a.m.

The sun is just beginning to come up. The birds are singing their little hearts out and the fragrance of the flower gardens is like a sweet potion for joy and peace. I'm glad that Mama and Daddy won't be back until late tomorrow because I want to pretend all day.

4:00 P.m.

After breakfast I took a swim, then conked out on a lounge chair by the pool. I slept until Mrs. Jolettea called me on the intercom.

After lunch she asked me if I'd like to go to the Griffith Park Zoo or maybe Venice Beach. She said she was worried about me being alone so much. I lied that I liked being alone and that I had a huge and difficult report to get to Sister Mary on Monday. Mrs. Jolettea said I was a "good child," and I apologized about her and her husband having to spend their weekend here to babysit me instead of being able to go to their own home for the weekend, as they usually do.

Sunday, March 21

The day is passing too quickly. I really wanted to talk to Jennifer, so I finally asked Mrs. Jolettea if I could ask her over. At first Mrs. Jolettea was hesitant, but then she said yes. I was so excited, I gave her a big hug and jumped for the phone.

Jennifer's brother drove her over, and the two of us reveled in having the morning to ourselves. We talked and swam, talked and played tennis, talked and just lounged like lazy cats in the sun. We'd had such a fantastically wonderful night on Friday that we had to keep pinching each other to be sure we weren't still dreaming.

Just before noon Jennifer suggested we ask Mrs. Jolettea if we could have Mark and David over for an hour or so. At first she said absolutely not! Then when she saw our sad faces, she said she didn't see how that could hurt if we, at all times, stayed where she could see us!

We stumbled over each other getting to the phone and within twenty minutes, Mark and David were at our gate with their bathing suits and tennis shoes in their hands.

Never has God created a nicer day, and when Mrs. Jolettea called us from the main house and said the boys had been there for almost three hours, we couldn't believe it.

Both guys came from good families so they immediately got their things together and started toward Mark's car. All four of us seemed kind of downcast until Mark said, "Hey gang, it's not like there isn't going to be a tomorrow!"

We all laughed at that and said how grateful we were for the telephone.

David said he would be on the phone the minute he got in his house. Mark took a smart-aleck stance and pulled his cell phone out of his pocket and said he'd be on my phone as soon as I got in my house.

What a funny, happy, appreciative group we are!

8:20 P.M.

Maybe soon Daddy and Mama will realize that I am no longer a little kid and that I deserve to go to movies and to the mall and the beach and do stuff with my friends.

My dear, dear, sweet, sweet Daddy would love both Mark and David if he knew them and saw what nice, honorable, good students from good families they are.

Daddy loves me and I know he wants me to be happy and well adjusted. In just one month I'll be sixteen, and in two months Jennifer will be sixteen. She knows her parents will give her a big party . . . but mostly with relatives and their friends. I hope they will invite me and Mark and David. I'm almost sure about me, but David and Mark? Hmmm . . .

I wonder if I'll even be able to have a party at all.

Isn't it strange how sometimes life can be so good, yet sometimes it can be so painful?

9:47 P.M.

Mama and Daddy just drove in. They were both exhausted, especially Mama. She was still standing beautifully straight and tall, and her green eyes looked like they were taking in the whole world, but she didn't talk. She simply gave me the tiniest smile and walked into her bedroom with Daddy's help. I'm concerned about her! Does she need a different doctor? A different therapist? A different surrounding? A different husband, who doesn't just treat her like she is a trophy wife? Maybe it's a different daughter she needs, or no daughter *at all*.

When Daddy came out of Mama's room he completely ignored me. I could feel my heart crumbling like potato chips. How could he not like me when he had been so happy and wonderful with me? What had I done? I want to kill myself! Nobody gives a damn about me! Not even me! Especially not me!

I'm going to bed to try to escape into sleep land.

Monday, March 22
6:00 a.m.

I was just awakened by a soft tapping at my door, and I jumped out of bed wondering what kind of horrible catastrophe was waiting for me now. But it wasn't a catastrophe, it was Daddy just inviting me to go out to an early breakfast with him. He said he'd be waiting for me in the library and for me to hurry up.

7:00 a.m.

I don't know when I've ever showered, dressed, or fixed my hair so fast. When I dashed into the library, Daddy was all smiles, and he took me into his arms and hugged me like he never wanted to let go. Then he pushed me away and, holding me by the shoulders as he looked at me, he told me that I was the most beautiful human being alive, that even in my silly little Catholic school outfit I looked good enough to eat, and he started nibbling my ear. He also told me, as we drove to Uncle John's Pancake House, that my fresh beauty and poise had now surpassed Mama's! I couldn't believe that and looked at him cautiously to see if he was kidding. He wasn't! I could see he wasn't and my heart throbbed with joy and pride. It was too wonderful for me to believe.

We sat in a little back corner booth, and Daddy told me what a "stoned rag" Mama had been in San Francisco and how he had almost been ashamed of her. Then he held my hand and told me how much he wished I had been there instead of her. I felt like a fantastic fairy princess who had just broken out of her ugly shell.

All the way home he continued to tell me nice things

about myself. I tried to snuggle up to him but he laughed and told me we would snuggle at home but in public people might think he had a gorgeous new girlfriend. He poked me in the arm playfully and said, "We don't want that in the *National Enquirer*, do we?"

I giggled and sat up straight and proper.

When we got home he hugged me, kissed me, and told me I was the most important thing in his life and that I should always remember that! Then he told me that around Mama he had to kind of ignore me because she was dangerously jealous of me.

As I waited for my school van I wondered how Mama could be jealous of me! What could that mean, and how should I treat Mama from now on? Maybe I should just stay away from her as much as I could.

It was kind of difficult to concentrate in school with all the wonderful loving things from Daddy rolling around in my head . . . and the scary things about Mama, like her never liking me or wanting me. That loaded me down with strangeness.

I wish I could talk to Mama's therapist about that, but of course I can't. I wondered for a while if I could talk to Jennifer or Mark, but that wouldn't work, either. It would just make me seem like a superweird kid from a superweird family.

Why has Mama always hated me? I thought I used

to remember her hugging me and rocking me and taking me on walks though the garden where we looked for little bugs and shiny rocks. I thought I remembered her buying me pretty dresses and taking me to the pony park and stuff. Wishful thinking I guess, or day-dreaming.

I wish Daddy hadn't told me how mean Mama had been to me when I was little and that that was why he had lost his temper with her and was sometimes violent. I don't blame him now that I know the circumstances! How could he not have done bad things to her when she was all the time doing bad things to me? And wouldn't it be miraculously amazing if maybe I can become a part of his life? Oh! I do hope with all my heart that I can!

• • •

Mama's personal maid is like a white old ghoul who disappears into the woodwork when I come near. I think she is kind of a maid-nurse because she stays very close to Doctor Barjoun when he's here.

I wish Daddy would get another doctor for Mama because Doctor Barjoun is scary! He's so hairy he looks like an ape-man, and he's never once, in all the times he's been here, looked me straight in the eye. Sister Mary says people who won't look you in the eye usually have a problem! He's like a character out of an old-fashioned scary movie. Mama doesn't need him;

she needs someone who is kind and gentle and fun and funny, someone who will encourage her to open her drapes and let the world's wonders come in. Someone to help her get her life back to normal.

I wonder what would happen if I went into Mama's room sometimes when she wasn't sleeping and I told her how wonderful and great she really is, not just beautiful on the outside but beautiful on the inside, too.

Once we had a lady come to school and talk to us about the person inside. Maybe Mama wouldn't be jealous of me if . . . imagine this . . . insignificant me trying to change the world . . . I don't think so! But I wish that I could!

Wednesday, March 24

Today Daddy was sitting out in the pool house when I got home from school. He yelled at me to pop upstairs and put on my swimsuit so we could play some waterball. I blew him a kiss and quickly changed my clothes.

It was a fun few hours with us playing our hearts out. Daddy was constantly telling me that he was trying to make up for all the hugs and kisses and loving that we had missed over the years. We really were physical, and in some little way I felt embarrassed because I wasn't really a little child anymore. I will be *sixteen* in a couple of weeks after all.

11:45 p.m.

I just woke up from dreaming that I was having *my* birthday party at *my* house. It was kind of strange because lots of girls from school were there, but only two boys, Mark and David. I wondered why I hadn't asked them to bring some of their guy friends.

Now that I'm completely awake, I wonder what would happen if I asked Daddy if I could have my birthday party here and invite a few boys as well as girls.

I've thought about it and thought about it and . . . what is the worst thing that could happen? He could say no. I think I'll ask sometime when he's feeling very mellow. Do I dare? Of course I dare! Daddy often tells me that we can talk about anything at all!

I'm excited! Excited almost out of my skin but, wouldn't you know, tonight would be one of the nights Daddy will be gone. Maybe by tomorrow I will have lost my courage to ask.

Thursday, March 25

Daddy's been gone both last night and tonight. If I don't ask him soon, it's going to be too late to send out invitations and buy party stuff.

I wonder if I could ask Mama? Just kind of talk

about it because I've never had a real birthday party before. We've always gone out to dinner at some fancy place, and once we flew to Catalina Island, just the three of us, but it's not like being with your friends, especially when you are a teenager.

Friday, March 26

I went out and picked a big bouquet of Mama's favorite yellow roses and tiptoed into her room. She moved slightly, sniffed, then opened her eyes. "For me, baby?" she said softly. "You picked them for me?" She said it like it was an earth-shattering gift from the gods. I felt guilty. I couldn't ever remember having given her a gift before. Daddy always piled up the gifts before us. I put the vase on Mama's night table and picked up her hand. Her skin was softer than anything I had ever touched before in my life, and the smile on her face was like I had given her my soul.

Huge tears welled up in her eyes and she whispered, "You don't hate me?"

I didn't have any idea what she was talking about, so I scrunched over on her bed and hugged her and kissed her like I'd wanted to do for years and years but hadn't dared. She had seemed so . . . something I couldn't comprehend . . . like there was a great stone wall between us, like there is around our house.

"What ever made you think I hated you?" I asked after a few seconds. Then memories of us picking flowers and finding bugs and riding ponies at the pony farm began coming back. Happy, breathless things were flooding into my mind on top of each other; good, wonderful, lovely times that had been completely blotted out of my mind. How could that have ever happened? But none of that stuff mattered now because she loves me! And I love her! We love each other!

Long, long ago something terrible must have estranged us . . . but it didn't matter what it was now because we had passed it!

I snuggled up beside Mama in her bed and we both cried about the years we had lost. Why? Why? Why???

After a little while, Mama got up and dressed and we walked down to the patio. Mama's nurse, Gretchen, had stuck her head into the room a couple of times but had hurriedly disappeared again. I was glad because she looked and acted like scary death warmed over. We didn't need that!

Cook brought breakfast out on the patio and we ate and talked and laughed. I felt like I was in heaven.

Mama told me I was the most beautiful person she had ever seen, and I said the same about her. She was almost as touchy and huggy as Daddy, and I felt warm and wanted.

We were so busy finding out about each other's thoughts and needs and wants that I almost missed my school van. I really wanted to miss it, but the old, sad Mama said, "Daddy wouldn't like that." The lights went off inside both of us, and we were like scared little-kid strangers again.

School was like hell. (Sorry, but there is no other way to explain it.) I couldn't concentrate, and Sister Mary thought I was just goofing off! I wasn't! I truly was trying my very hardest, but the mixed messages that were banging around in my mind were driving me crazy. How could Daddy be sometimes wonderful and loving and confidence-building and other times be a completely out-of-control maniac, wildly ranting and raving and . . . I tried to wipe the pictures away, but they wouldn't disappear.

Of course, Sister Mary couldn't understand or read my horrifying, appalling thoughts, so she tapped me across my hands with her soft ruler. In a way, it felt good, actually. It sort of centered me between what was happening in my life and what I was daydreaming would be happening in the future.

I often wonder if I am the only person in the world who feels like I do. Physically I have everything I want, and mentally I should be getting everything I need from the nuns. Still I feel like a lost soul, being picked and pulled from all sides, bounced and bruised, never knowing what the next few minutes or tomorrow will bring.

Some of the girls at school envy me. If they only knew! Or maybe their homes are like mine and they, too, just keep things hidden from the outside world.

I hurt so much that I feel like I am drowning in my own tears. How can I be so lost and lonely in my own body?

• • •

Daddy came home at about the same time my school van pulled up. He was the old, funny, make-me-happy Daddy, bringing gifts and ecstatic stories. At first I felt like a traitor to Mama when we played tennis and hugged and kissed each time we did something really well! And when he told me wonderful confidence-building things about myself, I didn't want to think about anything else!

After a little while, I got a kink in my thigh, and Daddy gave me a massage. I'd never had a deep one like that before and it felt totally wonderful. Daddy was so pleased he said he'd give me a massage as often as I wanted. I giggled and said, "How about three or four times every day?" Then I felt uncomfortable, so I jumped up and said I'd race him to the house.

He beat me to the patio, of course, and we both sprawled out on chairs huffing and puffing. After a bit he called Cook and asked her to bring out some refreshments.

As we sat there and talked Daddy seemed to be getting more and more mellow. I finally thought that I could talk to him about my having a birthday party here with kids from school and a "few others." I wasn't quite ready to mention "boys."

At first, Daddy seemed very happy about it. Then he looked sad and said he had made arrangements at the nicest hotel in San Francisco. He bit his lip and tried to pretend that his plans didn't matter, but I could see that he was hurt. He had booked a small private dining room overlooking the bay for us and a couple of San Francisco friends. He'd chartered a yacht for one day and also talked to Sister Mary about my taking two days off from school.

There weren't real tears in his eyes, but I could see that he felt like I would have felt if I'd made a big thing out of his birthday and then he'd just blown me off.

I jumped out of my chair and sat on his lap and hugged him and kissed his cheek. I wouldn't hurt him for anything, especially not now that he is taking anger management classes and he has become more mellow! I think . . . I hope . . .

I kissed him again and told him my birthday was no big deal, and that I really hadn't given it much thought at all.

Lie! Big, big lie!

I've been pretending again, writing down names of guests and colors for the tablecloths, making a menu that kids would like, checking on small bands, and what I'm going to wear, etc.

I'm glad Daddy got an important phone call exactly when he did because I was about to be torn in half. Now I've got to practice pretending that Daddy's San Francisco birthday gift is the greatest gift in the world . . . which, of course, it isn't! But I can't hurt him! I won't!

Thursday, April 1

I cried all last night! I had been so looking forward to having Mark and David and Jennifer and all the other kids over. I'd really spent a lot of time thinking about decorations and things. I knew Mr. and Mrs. Jolettea and Cook would do anything for me. In my mind I could still see the colored lights hanging around the tennis court and the cabana, and the band playing, and me dancing with Mark every single dance! Well, maybe not every dance. We'd need some time for wandering around the yard and through the house, even though I knew Daddy would have plenty of chaperones around.

I feel so empty inside, sort of like a hollow person with all their brain functioning and physical attributes out of whack. I don't know how I'm ever going to go to school. Sister Mary will think I'm on drugs or something. Maybe I can play sick. Play sick! I really am sick, sick of never being allowed to be the real me.

10:05 P.M.

I lived through today and I really didn't think I would. Twice I started crying for no reason at all, and Sister Mary came and comforted me. She really is a wonderful, wonderful, thoughtful person, and I love her. I really do! And I'll never look at her negatively again!

When I got home, I hurried into Mama's room. She was waiting for me, all dressed and sitting in a chair reading. It was like the old Mama in the back of my mind; make believe or real I didn't know, but I didn't care.

We talked about school and how I felt, and about Daddy's two-day surprise birthday party for me in San

Francisco, that now wouldn't be a surprise at all!

Mama was so caring and sweet that she almost made me feel normal again. It's healing and restoring to have a comforter. I am so glad she's getting better . . . or off the drugs or whatever the evil half-man, half-ape doctor and his ghoul nurse are giving her. Someday soon I'm going to beg Daddy to get rid of both of them and get a nice know-what-they-are-doing doctor, like Dr. Phil on TV, so Mama can become her old real self again.

Friday, my birthday! April 16
7:10 P.M.

My birthday party in San Francisco was fun, but not what I really had wanted! We did all the San Francisco things: cable cars, Chinatown, Fisherman's Pier, and Alcatraz Prison, the island where the country's most dangerous prisoners were kept in the old days.

I loved being on the yacht—the wind blowing my hair and the fragrance of saltwater occasionally splashing as we roller-coasted over a big wave.

Mama had stayed at the hotel. Daddy had told her he thought she should. He and I loved the excitement of it all. We went way out, far from land, and did some fishing, putting bait on hooks, catching and gutting.

The baiting and gutting I didn't like, but Daddy said I needed to learn how, so I did it. Yuck!

We even saw some sharks and other fish that were almost flying up out of the water.

We gave the fish we had caught to a couple of workers on the boat. Two of the fish were huge, and Daddy had to help me reel the monster I caught in.

While Daddy was taking a nap on the deck, I pretended Mark and Jennifer and David were with us. We were running all over the boat and playing games, diving off the boat into the water and chasing dolphins, etc. Daddy tried hard, but he couldn't ever be a kid again! I wish he could understand that! Adults are funny that way.

Saturday, April 17

Last night was the most horrible night of my life. After dinner, Daddy asked Mama if she would like to stay in the hotel. She said she would. Daddy asked if she was sure about that and she said she was. I wanted her to come with us to see the night side of San Francisco but what Daddy even intimated was what Mama and I did!

Daddy had had a few drinks during dinner, and I wasn't really comfortable around him. But I had no choice. . . .

As were riding in the limo from one gross place to another even more crude, vulgar place, I wanted to throw up.

I knew Daddy had been drinking heavily or he wouldn't ever have taken me to places like that. I wished I could get him to drink soda like I was, but nobody tells Daddy what to do!

I thought I'd explode if I drank any more soda, but while I went to the ladies' room, Daddy ordered another one for me and I took a few sips just to please him. I was feeling woozy and wondering what was happening when Daddy suddenly grabbed me in a real hurting way. I started crying and tried to pull away but Daddy just laughed.

After a little while the music seemed to get louder and the lights brighter and flashing faster and faster in bright colors. People were . . . it wasn't really dancing. It was too obscene for words, and my beautiful dress was being torn to shreds.

Pictures of Sister Mary and Sister Martha and the other nuns raced on top of each other through my blurred mind as we all seemed to be sinking together down to hell. I tried to scream, "Help . . . help . . . help," but the sounds were blurred and getting fainter.

Two giant men came from nowhere and pulled me away from Daddy and wrestled him to the floor. A waiter was holding me up while Daddy screamed and cursed and threatened and lashed out at them with his arms and legs. Finally they overpowered him and went through his pockets and found our hotel card.

From way out in space I could hear someone say, "We can put this perp in a cab and send him back to the hotel, but what about the girl? She has to be way under age." I heard someone, in the far fuzzy distance saying, "Get rid of both of them. I don't care where they go."

Then someone put me in a cab.

I woke up in my hotel room and thought I had had a horrible nightmare.

Another picture of pious Sister Mary and the other nuns flashed through my mind, and I was almost sure Daddy and I had both gone to hell. I'd heard enough about that in my many years of Catholic school. We had to have been in hell!

I didn't know what time it was or what day it was when Daddy woke me up and told me to shower and get dressed. I pretended nothing had happened, but I think Daddy was so drunk last night he couldn't remember. I certainly don't want Mama to know anything.

When I got out of the shower, I noticed the clothes I had worn last night were gone. It was beyond scary! A sensation of oppression and helplessness swept over me, boxed me in, imprisoned me!

Slowly I managed to, with great effort, dress, fix my hair, and brush my teeth. All of it seemed like an automatic reflex.

Time passed and Mama knocked on my door and asked if I was ready for breakfast. That seemed strange because Mama rarely, if ever, eats breakfast.

We walked to the elevator and then to the dining room without saying a word to each other.

At probably the most ostentatious table in the luxurious skyroom, Daddy sat like he was a deity. He stood up when he saw us and helped us to our seats. Then he began talking about our boat trip and all the other things . . . except what had happened last night. Mama and I both knew by the look on his face that we were never to mention that incident again, ever!

I pretended to sleep on our way home. Having my brain rattling with the good things that might have been on my birthday! Poor, poor Daddy was drugged and drunk. I'm sure he didn't even remember what had happened.

Monday, May 10

It's been almost four weeks since the San Francisco thing, and I know Daddy is really sorry. He's been treating both me and Mama like we are queens. I know Daddy was under the influence of something, otherwise he would never, never, never have taken me to that place.

Tuesday, May 11

It's so wonderful to be home in our nice safe place and have Jennifer coming over to study and play tennis and swim, like it was before San Francisco! It's even more wonderful to spend long periods talking to Mark. He tells me all about his schoolwork and after-school things. He also tells me about his parents and brothers, and they seem so funny and always happy. I can't wait to meet them. But there is a little scared place inside me that worries about his parents and them liking me as much as I like them.

Oh please, please Holy Father, and Mary, Mother of Jesus, help me and forgive me and heal me. Make me clean again!

Wednesday, May 12

The birds are beginning to sing again and the sun is beginning to shine. God is with me and I am in many ways semi-happy, but for some cold, scary reason I can't be at all comfortable around Daddy. I don't know what I will ever do if he wants me to go out to dinner with him or even play tennis or swim. I felt even before we went to San Francisco that he was getting much too physical. Or is it me? Have the nuns brainwashed me into thinking all right things are wrong?

Oops . . . the phone . . . see ya.

• • •

It was Mark and he really wants to see me again. Some of his friends are coming to a Lecture Meeting Party on Friday night. Melek, Mark's friend, is bringing his father, a very important doctor who works with stem cells. David says he's so intelligent that he's off the charts, but he's also funny and entertaining. Then we will dance and play games and stuff, and of course eat. We talked for the longest time about the funny-sounding Lecture Meeting Party, and my heart longs to go, but . . .

Oops . . . phone again. I hope it's Jennifer! Mark said David was going to call her, and I didn't want to tie up her line, so I've been nervously waiting.

• • •

I can't believe this! Jennifer's parents are going to let her go to Mark's party! Her dad knows a lot about Mark's dad's business and has even done some things with him. Jennifer cooed like a four-year-old. They are going to let their bitty baby girl go to the party with boys, but her big brothers will have to take her there and bring her back. She said a nasty phrase then that would have kept her home from parties for the rest of her life! I shivered and hoped that no member of her family was on the line.

• • •

I called Mark back and told him I could come. He was elated. I was scared! How? How could I ever manage to get out of the house and back in while Mama and Daddy were there? Could I bribe Cook or maybe Mr. Jolettea to smuggle me out and smuggle me back in again? That would be dangerous, but . . .

2:37 a.m.

I've finally decided that the only possible way for me to get to the party is to use the emergency rope fire ladder again. It's big and it's heavy, but I gotta do what I gotta do!

Jennifer is pretty sure her oldest brother, Steve, will help me. He knows me well from being at their house, and Jennifer has told him often about how strict my parents are. That would take me straight to the rainbow. I'm so happy I'm about to pop right here in my bed!

Tuesday, May 18

I woke up dreaming that Mark and I were dancing to a slow song. He was holding me gently and sweetly . . . not like a cannibal that wanted to eat me! That wasn't a nice thing to say about Daddy and hopefully I'll never feel that way again, but . . . Sometimes he does scare me, and I wish he would send me to a convent! But . . . I don't know . . . I'm so mixed up and lost inside myself. If Mama didn't have such a crazy therapist, I'd ask him how loony I am and if I'll ever get myself together.

Three days till I see Mark!

The sun is up and the sprinklers are on and the birds are singing their hearts out, just for me. Mark said last night on the phone that I was the only girlfriend he had ever had, and then we laughed about the few stolen hours we'd ever had together. Mark hates it that we had to lie. I hate it, too, but I know my daddy better than he does!

Mark often talks about wanting to talk to Daddy or send him a long letter or something.

He even once mentioned that he would like to invite my parents over to meet his parents. Little did he know! But then little did I know about his parents except that from what he said they seemed even nicer and kinder and more thoughtful than Jennifer's, if that's possible.

Wednesday, May 19

I called Mark after school today. He wasn't there but his mother was. She seemed so thoughtful and kind that I instantly felt comfortable with her, which is really uncommon for me! I'm totally suspicious of everyone! She told me that Mark talked about me often and how happy she was that he had met a nice girl who had an optimistic, sunshiny attitude about life, education, and all the other things that mattered.

I hadn't had any idea how dysfunctional my family was until I met Jennifer and Mark. And I am happy about going to the Lecture Meeting Party.

Thursday, May 20

Today I could hardly concentrate on anything at school! My mind was sloshing around about what I was going to wear and how I'd fix my hair and how I'd sneak out and back in again, especially carrying the heavy emergency fire ladder. It is mostly made of rope, but it is still really heavy! I know! From carrying it both out and in the last time!

I almost had an electric shock of fear that shot me off my chair. What if? There were so many "what ifs" that my brain was scrambled like eggs. It's scary as anything, but I can't not go! Neither can I stop thinking about Daddy and me in the pool and in the car, and me sitting on his lap and kissing his face. I had been doing it like a tiny kid starved for love and attention, wanting to be wanted and petted and hugged, not wanting what I think maybe he wanted. No. No.

No! That's disgusting! Evil and disgusting! I'm his daughter! Please . . . please God forgive me for ever thinking that!

Friday, May 21

I've been reconsidering going to Mark's Lecture Meeting Party. At first I thought I couldn't go. Now I know I have to! This may be the last time that I'll get to do anything with anybody my age until I'm in college. I hope it won't be a Catholic college.

At least for tonight I'm going to blank out all the negative things in my head and concentrate on each moment of, possibly, the last happy day in my existence!

The thought that if Daddy finds out about tonight he might make me become a nun flashed through my mind. Is that possible? I wonder how old one has to be to become a nun. I've seen a couple of nuns who seemed very young.

I've demanded my mind not to allow in it anything negative. Tonight I am going to be Cinderella going to the ball and . . . whatever comes after that?! So be it!

7:30 P.M.

I'm all ready to go and just waiting for the right time to sneak out to the rock wall with the ladder. And, you know, as I think about Daddy, he isn't the evil one with the evil thoughts. It's me! He was drunk and probably drugged by some of those crazy losers. He wasn't really responsible! Could that be? Yes, it could be! And it was! I'm absolutely, positively sure it was! Now I feel a lot better!

11:50 P.m.

The lecture about stem cells was absolutely mind boggling, and I can't believe how much of the information I've retained. In fact, I think I'll write a paper on the subject for school.

Never have I had such a lovely time in my life. Mark's parents are as wonderful and loving and caring as he is! And so were all the other people there! I really felt like I had died and gone to heaven, and I wanted, with every pore in my body, to have each person there to be my favorite, happy and fun, yet serious, forever friend!

After the lecture, we danced for a little while, then ate and played the funniest and most fun game in the world. Everyone else there had played it but me. I had a hard time keeping up for a couple of minutes then I decided that charades is the coolest game in the world. Even if it is an oldie!

1:30 a.m.

It's late . . . or maybe early . . . but I still can't go to sleep. I'm much too excited for that! Actually I'm really loving reliving every moment of Mark's party. How blessed I am to have been there and how easily I managed to get the emergency fire ladder back where it belongs—*thank goodness!*

I will never forget Mark's kiss. He and I were going to get another box of eclairs to put on the table but . . . in the breezeway he stopped me and we just sort of pulled together like we were magnetized. His kiss was sweet and gentle, and he touched my face and hair like I was something breakable. I thought I'd swoon, like old-fashioned ladies do in the educational movies we see at school.

I have never been so happy and felt so belonging in the human race.

• • •

Daddy just knocked at my door and told me to slip on some shorts and a shirt, that he wanted to talk to me. He didn't sound mad . . . thank goodness. . . . Is it Mama? I'd better hurry.

Daddy gave me two big white candies and almost immediately I felt myself evaporating . . .

But I wanted more of the strange candies! More and more! And more!

Light years later???

I am really on another planet . . . or . . .

Once upon a time, ages and ages ago, Sister Mary

tried to explain hell to us: "Satan's place of everlasting fire, underworld purgatory, bottomless pit," etc. . . .

Now I know! I'm there! I can smell the unimaginable stench and feel the gut-wrenching degradation.

Possibly I've gone crazy! Maybe I'm in the black bottomless pit!

I just woke up on a hard little bed, surrounded by other ragged, dirty-looking, smelly, nonhuman creatures just like me. Some were snoring, some crying, some others were shaking with fear, having horrendous nightmares or hangovers or . . . whatever . . .

Thank . . . I was going to write "God," but I'm not sure anymore that there is a God. Maybe I'm not even thankful that I'm alive anymore.

How did I get here?

I must write down every single thing. . . .

Why? Who cares? No one!

No one could want to have anything to do with me now . . . but writing is all I've got to keep me together. Do I even want to be kept together?

Yes.

No.

Yes, no, yes, no, no, no, no.

Most of me wants to drop out of this black, scary hellhole at any cost, but one little part of me wants to hang on. The scared, wimpy, used-to-be-trusting, wanting-love-and-attention, idiot part of me.

When I first came into this flea- and lice-infested flop house for the throw-away creatures who were no longer human beings, I wondered how I could kill myself.

Now some scared little something inside of me wants to talk to Jason, the young man who found me on the street and took me in.

When I got here he asked me what I wanted and I said some paper and a pencil. He laughed, patted me on the head like a child, and brought me a notebook, a pencil, and a huge semihard roll that tasted like manna from heaven, if there is a heaven. I'm so in all ways confused! Heaven? Hell? Right? Wrong?

Life . . . death . . . please, somebody help me. Please . . . please . . . please . . .

● ● ●

A little morning light is beginning to peek in through the cracked glass window on the other side of the room, and people are beginning to stir around me. I'm shivering so much that my whole rickety cot is shaking! What will be the next step for me?

I want . . . no, I desperately need to talk to Jason, but he's busy helping get the breakfast things out.

What to do?

The overhead lights are on now, and all the reject people are straggling out to eat. Ugggh . . . even the thought of food makes me want to throw up.

How did I ever get from there to here?

It's a horrible unbelievable nightmare!

Maybe I'll wake up eventually.

At some time, in another life, I was in my everything-I-ever-wanted room, in my beautiful, clean, good-smelling bed, going over the loveliest time I had ever had with Mark. . . .

Then Daddy was knocking and telling me to get up, put on some shorts and a shirt, and to hurry quietly downstairs.

As I came to the bottom landing Daddy put his finger to his mouth and whispered, "Come out to the car and I'll tell you where we are going."

I hopped into the gardener's old truck with Daddy, wondering why he would ever drive the gardener's truck instead of his Mercedes or one of his other cars, and why he would ever wear an old cap that looked like it was the gardener's. He seemed so focused on whatever he was thinking that I squeezed closer to him and patted his arm. Almost automatically his hand flopped up and hit me on the side of the head so hard I was stunned. Then he started calling me a "ho" and a "slut" and every other vile and vulgar thing he could think of, plus lots of words I'd never heard before.

"No, no Daddy," I whispered, "I'm none of those things. I'm a virgin and I've only been kissed once by a boy."

Daddy called me more unspeakable obscene names

and hit me again. This time he was so angry and out of control that he almost ran into another car coming in the opposite direction. The man in that car honked his horn and called Daddy bad names. I wanted to jump out of the car but Daddy was driving too fast and I was too scared.

I tried again to explain but Daddy wouldn't listen! He was obsessed by the ladder over the fence and me sneaking out. He accused me of the vilest things in the world. I was mentally and morally beaten to shreds, and half the time I didn't even know what he was talking about.

Daddy had been driving around in circles but then he slowed down and started heading toward Hollywood Boulevard. How did we get there? I wanted and needed more candies! I really did!

My heart almost stopped! I didn't know the strange person who was driving the gardener's truck and wearing the gardener's cap! I couldn't believe what I was hearing and was sure I was feeling and thinking things that weren't true . . . couldn't be true.

Daddy turned off Hollywood Boulevard on a dark, dirty little street where he said hookers hang out. I wondered why he would take me to a place like that and tell me about kids, some eleven and twelve years old, who had run away to glamorous Hollywood and were now selling their bodies because they didn't have anything else to sell.

I couldn't understand what was going on in his mind. Was he trying to scare me into being a good girl? I tried to tell him he didn't have to do that because the nuns had already hammered that stuff into our heads, but he wasn't listening. It was as if he was deaf.

When we got close to a girl who looked like a frightened little child, Daddy held out a twenty-dollar bill. At first she looked like she was going to run away, then she grabbed Daddy's hand with the money in it and got into the truck.

Quickly he kicked her out and slammed on the gas. He said, "Forget her! I'm going to take you where you belong!"

What is going to happen to me now? Obviously Daddy doesn't want me anymore and Mama is a drug addict. Neither of them ever mentioned even one person in either of their families. Where will I go? What will I do?

• • •

As Daddy turned on Wilshire Boulevard, toward downtown Los Angeles, I sat frozen with fear. He told me that he had, at first, meant to leave me on Hollywood Hooker Way with the rest of the blank, blank, blank that I can't even write. But then he had thought of something better and was going to take me down to Skid Row, in the bowels of Los Angeles, and see how I'd fend for myself there.

When we got to Skid Row, I couldn't believe it! It was like a terrible movie set. Drunken men stretched against buildings; black-eyed, bloody, beaten women stumbling out of bars; two men screaming and cursing at the cars that passed by.

Daddy snickered as he unlocked my side of the car and pushed me out the door.

Completely out of control I whimpered, "But Daddy, I don't have any shoes, I'm bare-footed and . . ."

He laughed and drove off. I shivered and in some stupid, scared way hoped that he'd come back and pick me up.

• • •

After a forever of forevers, a frightening old man wobbled up and offered to share his bottle of liquor. Automatically I said, "I have AIDS! I have AIDS!" like people in the bible used to call out, "Leper, leprosy" when strangers came around them. The old man hurried away, looking afraid and repulsed.

Some days and nights passed, and I hid behind garbage Dumpsters, shivering in the cold night air with only dirty newspapers to cover me. My fingernails were broken off from scavenging Dumpsters for food, my bare feet were cut and bruised, and vermin crawled inside and outside my clothes. Rats and/or mice scurried around. There was nothing to drink! It was pure hell!

Once a police car came by and I waved and tried to stop it, but I guess the policeman didn't care about me.

I stunk so much I could hardly stand myself. And I was so hungry and thirsty I decided the only thing for me to do would be to run out in front of the next big truck that drove by! I didn't know where I'd been—or what? And I was running out of candy!

Knowing that I'd have to do some explaining to God before I killed myself, and hoping that He would understand, I kneeled in the shadows to pray. I had hardly started when I felt a hand on my shoulder. I sensed that the hand was gentle and the voice of the young man who was helping me up was comforting. He said he was from the Salvation Army Rescue House and this was his mission, to save people from the wicked streets.

I started crying uncontrollably and cried all the way to the mission.

Jason walked close to me down the dark streets and begged me not to kill myself, but I couldn't see any other way out, and it seemed like I'd seen him before.

At the shelter Jason got me some clean clothes and led me to a shower. But I can't stay at the Salvation Army shelter forever. Daddy would say this is where I belong! But at least it's not like what the kids, both boys and girls, have to go through on Hollywood Hooker Way. That is so sad and horrible that I don't think I'll ever stop crying inside, and my candy is all gone! Candy? No! Drugs!

Jason stopped by to see how I was doing after a while and he's the most beautiful person I've ever met. He cares about the people here; the young and the old, the sturdy and the weak. He's embarrassed that he looks so different, with strange crinkled red skin all over the right side of his face and on his right hand, but inside he's like God meant everyone to be.

Since it was way past dinnertime, Jason brought me a roll and glass of milk, and I'll love him forever for that.

I'm kind of skipping back and forth on parts here, but anyway, early in the morning after breakfast, Jason said a lady wanted to talk to me. I was scared out of my skin. Talk to me about what? I hated lying but I could never, through all eternity, tell anyone the unthinkable things that had happened to me. Nor even the good things like Mark, Jennifer, David, the nuns, Mark's wonderful friends, and even Mrs. Jolettea and Cook. I thought about the running in front of the big truck again, maybe it *was* the only way out! I certainly didn't want to be sent back to Daddy.

I'd read about kids who had been abused by their parents and then had been sent back to them to have even more horrendous experiences.

Mama wouldn't, couldn't help me, and even the thought of Daddy . . . I felt like I had to throw up.

I want to die! I really, really, really do!

• • •

When Jason took my hand and led me into the lady's small office, I felt like I was going to be slaughtered, but she wasn't at all like that. She was more like Jason; kind and sweet and warm, wanting to keep me out of harm. She asked me how I'd become a "street kid" (not in those words of course) and I lied and told her I had amnesia. (Thank goodness I'd written a paper on that subject only a short time ago.) She believed me when I told her that I had had some kind of brain injury. I said I couldn't remember how or when I got it, just that I had partial or total loss of memory sometimes. She felt eventually, hopefully very soon, the injury, shock, or repression would heal, and told me I should have faith.

She asked me to call her Bailia and said she'd have a home for me in a day or two and for me to stay close to the Salvation Army shelter till then. I did that gladly!

The people in the shelter, including me, look and act like refugees from a starving third-world country . . . and it is really, really scary! Down to the bottom soles of my feet scary! I'm pretty sure a lot of them are either drunk, stoned, or crazy.

I am living in a nightmare reality that I will probably never wake up from! Please, please God take me away from all this!

Day ?

Mrs. Totter's cot is next to mine. In fact it is so close to mine that I can hear her soft breathing at night. It is almost like a kitten purring and it gives me comfort. She said her husband and two children had been killed in an automobile accident . . . but beyond that, she didn't seem to be able to talk about them. Maybe that is why she began to treat me like I was her own child. She told me about growing up in Kansas on a dairy farm with five brothers and two sisters, and how they had to walk almost three miles to school. She also told me about them sitting around the fireplace at night singing songs and telling stories about the interesting or funny things that had happened during the day.

Sometimes the family made taffy candy or popcorn and played jokes on each other. Everybody loved to play jokes. I envied their family even though they were "dirt poor."

I had things but they had love and protection!

Mrs. Totter's grammar is bad and she isn't neat or refined at all, but she hugged me and she wiped away my tears when I cried, and told me over and over again that everything would be all right. I'd never had that kind of true, I-came-first love, and it slightly defrosted my cold, suspicious, frozen heart.

Friday, I think

Today two sort of stern-looking ladies drove up to the Salvation Army shelter. Jason hurried me back into a corner and told me they had probably found a home for me. He gave me a good pep talk and I hugged him like the brother I'd never had.

The ladies took me into Bailia's dark little office and asked me a million questions. Most of the night before I'd stayed awake trying to figure out what I could possibly say, and I guess I did a pretty good job. They accepted all my lies about my amnesia and that I could only remember being hit on the head and the things that had happened since then, like walking and walking endlessly, and being scared until Jason picked me up and brought me to the shelter.

I didn't want to leave Mrs. Totter and Jason, but the ladies said they thought I would be very happy in my new home. I don't know why I ever told them that I was fourteen, instead of the sixteen I really am. I guess it was because I felt so young and vulnerable. Mrs. Totter hugged me and told me that if she had a place to go to she would take me. I clung to her like a baby until the ladies pulled me away. In the car they told me Mrs. Totter was mentally impaired and they were looking for a nursing home for her.

Another kick in the gut! Crazy old lady! She probably didn't even know what she was saying . . . but she seemed lucid. . . . Maybe she is and they just think she isn't! Like lots of times since the . . . you know thing . . . I'm almost sure I've gone wacky. I believe that can happen from stress and strain! Maybe my whole old life, as I remember it, is a crazy hodge-podge of things I've read or seen in movies or on TV.

All the way to my new home, the ladies were telling me about the rules I would have to live by and, if I didn't, they might have to put me in a juvenile kind of place that wouldn't be nearly as nice. They made it sound like a kids' jail.

What if I had told them the truth about Daddy being a big, powerful, important mogul, living in our huge locked-in, rock-walled estate? Would I be sent back to him with nobody believing me? Why would anyone in their right mind believe a kid as scatterbrained as I am, and how could they believe what had really happened, really did happen!

Besides, I know Daddy would go, first thing, to the nuns and they would confirm that he's right next to

Jesus; giving huge grants and gifts, helping people all over, saving the whales, etc.! Nobody in the whole world would not believe him!

● ● ●

It's the middle of the night.

I'm feeling terrible about Mama. I know she's addicted to who knows how many things. What is going to happen to her? Maybe I should tell the truth for her sake . . . but then what would happen to me?

I'm a wimp and a complete gutless wonder. I don't even deserve to breathe!

New Home

When I first got here I was like an automated person with no thinking abilities and systems of my own. I agreed with everything Mrs. Jackson and her husband said.

He is as fat and flubbery as she is skinny and precise. There are four other children in the house, all of them, like me, throw-away kids, I guess. Dick, the oldest kid, seems sulky and not real bright. Melba Lacy, who always has to be called "Melba Lacy," is so quiet and scared that I can relate to her on that level. Frankie, who the kids call "Frog" when the parent figures aren't around, is maybe eleven, and he does look like a frog with his big squashed-out eyes and huge lips.

Donita, a little black girl, I guess about three or four, cries and whines and hides in closets and under beds. Sometimes she stays so still and quiet it is as if she is dead; she has lots of scars and cigarette burns on her body.

• • •

Once, eons ago, I thought I was a lost soul. Now I know I am a lost soul. One that will probably be lost forever!

• • •

I'm so grateful that Jason stuffed a fat notebook into the little sack of things I took from the Salvation Army shelter. I don't know how I could ever live without being able to write.

Monday, May 31

I've been here three days and each day Donita wets her crib, then curls up into a hard little knot and whimpers like a cold injured animal. It drives Mrs. Jackson crazy, but she doesn't understand. Apparently Mrs. Jackson didn't wet her bed when she was little, or maybe she's just forgotten. I hate to hear Mrs. Jackson yell at Donita, as though that would make a difference. And Mrs. Jackson doesn't even change her bed, she just makes her sleep in the cold stinky wetness.

Today I asked Mrs. Jackson if I could rinse out

Donita's bedding and put it on the clothes line. She shrugged so I did it. I also cuddled Donita and sang some nursery songs to her. At first she was stiff and still as a board, but then she began to soften up some and I almost felt like her mother. It was a nice feeling. Obviously the little, almost baby kid has never had much good stuff in her life.

I hope she had a nice feeling about the cuddling and singing like I did. I do deeply hope so, because she always looks like something is about to gobble her up, skin, bones, and all! She's especially scared of Mr. Jackson and often slightly wets her pants even when he comes near her. Dick and Frog giggle. Melba Lacy and I both feel sad.

Tuesday, July 13

It's mostly horrible living in this dirty house. I don't think anyone here really knows what "clean" is, or cares! I was told I could call Mrs. Jackson "Mother" or "Mom" but nobody else does.

Dick bugs the life out of me. He always calls me "diarrhea head" when the adults aren't around. He says it's because my hair is the color of diarrhea. That really hurts. I hate even writing the word it's so gross and low class.

I hope Melba Lacy and I will be friends soon. She is

the Pollyanna of the house but no one appreciates her. In fact, Frog and Dick are sometimes cruel to her, both physically and verbally.

Monday, September 13

Today I'm going to a new school. I hope it isn't going to be like some of the schools I've seen in movies, like in ghettos and stuff. I don't want to go back to a fourteen-year-old status but I can't think of one single way to change that lie! I'm almost paralyzed with terror! My whole life is a lie, one I will probably never be able to get out of! Stupid, bungling, doing everything wrong me!

8:00 a.m.

A rickety bus picked up Dick, Melba Lacy, Frog, and me. Dick and Frog sat in the back row and were loud and crude. They pretended they didn't know Melba Lacy and me! We pretended we didn't know them!

The school, which is a long way away, is as dilapidated as the bus. They both smell of mold and other awful stinky things. The kids were all dressed in cheesy clothes, including me, and I guess I stunk, too. It was humiliating and I wanted like anything to disappear into thin air but . . . no way.

Melba Lacy is quite a bit younger than I am, but still

she acted like she was my new mother. She took me into the principal's office and introduced me, then scurried off to her class telling me she would meet me at the bus stop after school, in case our paths didn't cross before that.

The principal, Mrs. Pulsifer, hardly looked up at me she was so busy shuffling papers, finally she found the packet the people who had taken me from the Salvation Army had put together from my lies.

Without even looking up, Mrs. Pulsifer asked me if I was doing better with my "memory retention," then she explained "retention" as though I was a four-year-old. I wanted to spit in her face. Not really! But I felt so boxed in and at the same time shut out that my mind was whirling around like a blender.

Seeing how confused I was, Mrs. Pulsifer sat me at a little desk in the corner of her room and gave me a page of questions to answer. They were third-grade questions and I wanted to jump up and run away, but to where . . . ?

I reminded myself of selfless Melba Lacy and slowly the stress started running out of my pores like water dripping from a hose. Soon, I hoped, I'd find out more about her past. But not mine! I didn't want anyone to know about mine!

I finished Mrs. Pulsifer's question sheet in about two minutes, and she gave me a cold slice of a smile and handed me a sheet with fourth-grade questions.

I zipped that off and the next two, probably low fifth and sixth grade. Then I got worried. I couldn't let Mrs. Pulsifer, or anyone else, know that I'd always gone to the best schools money could buy, and had, as far back as I could remember, tutors and specialists in every subject.

At the seventh-grade level I began to make a number of mistakes on purpose, and chew on my pencil like Melba Lacy did when she was trying to do her lessons at home.

Mrs. Pulsifer asked me if I remembered my grade and I stammered and said, "No." The lies were eating me up inside but I couldn't conceive of any possible way to change the situation I'd created for myself.

"Would you like to try seventh grade?" Mrs. Pulsifer asked.

"Could I try eighth or ninth?" I asked, hardly daring to breathe.

"Hmmm . . . maybe eighth," Mrs. Pulsifer said as though she were talking to herself. Then she called someone to pick me up and take me to the eighth-grade class.

I am completely and eternally beaten both mentally and socially! I can see no way out! I am barely sixteen years old and all educational outlets in my life have been blocked. What am I to do? I cannot go back to the evil creature I once thought of as my daddy. And who would believe me when I can't even believe myself? Miserable, lying creature that I am! I am but a lying evil shadow of my old self, and probably will be for the rest of my life!

Thursday, September 16

Most of the kids in my eighth-grade class are the equivalent of uncaring retards. There is no discipline in the room, and no one seemed to be in the least bit interested in what they are supposed to be learning. Their grammar is terrible and their social skills . . . they probably don't even know what "social skills" are, or any of the other niceties in life. In a way, that makes me feel very sorry for them. How can they ever get good jobs or become something of importance, to themselves, or to humanity, in any way, if they haven't been taught!

I am really depressed! Really, really depressed! Life is worthless! And Dick is right about my hair!

Friday, September 17

Melba Lacy heard me crying in my sleep and climbed down from her top bunk. She shushed me and whispered for me to come sit out on the front porch steps so we could talk.

When I got there I couldn't talk. I was so full of lies

I'd completely forgotten how to communicate. But that didn't seem to matter to Melba Lacy at all. She held my hand and told me how she had always wanted to become a painter or a schoolteacher or a writer, and how she had always lived a life of almost complete pretend.

After her mama ran off with a man who worked in her office, her daddy started drinking all the time, leaving her alone for days in her cold, dark house, sometimes with little or no food. One day she found her little kitty, Whitey, dead on her bed. Screaming in terror, she picked up Whitey and carried her to the neighbors, even though her Daddy had told her they were terrible people and would hurt her a lot if she went there.

The neighbors were not terrible people; in fact they were the kindest, nicest people she had ever known. After the neighbors had helped her put little Whitey, who had probably died from hunger, in a semi-clean white box, they had a serious funeral for the little kitty and told Melba Lacy that Whitey had gone up to heaven to live with God and the angels.

Melba Lacy hadn't known much about God and angels, so I told her a lot, then said I'd tell her more another time.

We sat and watched the moon and stars for, I suspect, most of the night, because Melba Lacy had so much to tell me. She told me how her parents had screamed and fought as long as she could remember. Her daddy didn't like her mother's parents, so they were never allowed to see them or even talk to them on the phone. One day her grandma did call, and her daddy beat up her mama terribly. It wasn't long after that that her mama just up and left. After "many, many weeks" Melba Lacy's daddy left, too.

Melba Lacy's nice neighbors tried to get in touch with her grandparents but they couldn't. Melba Lacy wanted to dig up Whitey and take him with her when she went into foster care, but the neighbors convinced her that they would always take good care of Whitey and that they would pray every night for Melba Lacy. Melba Lacy didn't know much about prayer, so we've got to talk about that in the future. Sometimes she reminds me of the old nun Sister Mary at my dear, precious Catholic girls' school.

Melba Lacy is always kind and concerned about others, also forgiving of bad things! Dick and Frog tease her unmercifully, sometimes even hit her and pull her hair and call her terrible names. She never tattles on them or tries to get them into trouble like I'd like to do. She just simply tries to positively and gently go with the flow of life.

I've been lying in bed thinking about how much better off I'd be if I were more like Melba Lacy.

Sometimes I get so frustrated by Dick and Frog that I almost explode. Then I hate myself and everybody else in the world. I cry myself to sleep with a big heavy pile of evil and hurt inside me, while little snippets of memories of Mark and Jennifer and poor addicted Mama and the dear, dear nuns, float around before my eyes.

Often, at times like tonight, I feel like I really have been sent to purgatory to stay forever and never be allowed to go back into the beautiful, wonderful days before . . .

> *Please stop*
> *dear tears.*
> *You're splashing*
> *in my ears.*
> *You're drowning*
> *both my heart*
> *and every other part*
> *of me,*
> *or what I want to be.*
> *I hate it here.*
> *There's fear*
> *and wondering.*
> *If I cry and cry and cry and cry,*
> *I'll die.*
> *I hope that's so.*

I want to go.
This life is hell.
There is no heaven.
There is no me!
I wish that that could be!

Tuesday, September 21

One more dreary day stacked upon another!

I'm in a class of kids who don't care about anything that is educational in any way. We don't have enough books to go around, and we don't have homework. Mrs. Lakin doesn't seem to care that there is absolutely no discipline in the class.

With almost a physical pain, I miss dear Sister Mary and the other nuns, who were trying to instruct us how to make something of ourselves. They were seriously encouraging us to respect English, math, music, science, ethics, etc., so that we could someday make the world a better place.

This school's library is almost like a closet, it is so small, and what books they have are old and dusty and torn. I wanted to take something home to study, but they don't even have a full set of encyclopedias or much of anything else. I had thought maybe I could help Melba Lacy with her schoolwork . . . but how? Maybe I'll have to find a way. She deserves that! And I am smart! *Am* I smart, or was I just a privileged student who was carefully and thoroughly and methodically indoctrinated?

Thursday, September 23

I was scared silly when I walked into the principal's office and asked if she could give me her old used paper that had one clean side. At first she seemed shocked, but when I told her about Melba Lacy and how I wanted to be her tutor, she smiled. I'd never seen a real smile on her face before, and as she picked up a pile of papers, she also stuck in a fresh new notebook. I wanted to hug her and she looked like she wanted to hug me. It was a wonderful feeling!

Tuesday, September 28

For the first few "eternity weeks" I was here, it seemed like time had stopped. Now it's flying by on "gossamer wings." I'm not exactly sure what that phrase means, but to me it means something very, very special. I have a reason for living. Before I felt useless and trashy and empty! Now I'm going to make Melba Lacy into a proper, educated young lady! We'll have to be careful not to go so far that the kids will tease us or anything. Melba Lacy said we can be like the nuns would want us to be inside, and like the kids in our school and home on the outside. We both laughed at that and it is our private wonderful thing! She's feeding my ego and I'm feeding hers. It's the most wonderful thing that has ever happened in my life except (maybe) Mark's party! But I can't allow myself to think about that . . . it's too close to Daddy's grossness and Mama's problems.

Monday, October 4

I can't believe how fast Melba Lacy is learning. She no longer says "ain't" or any of the other unacceptable words that were so much a part of her vocabulary. We go out by the trees at night after everyone else is in bed and I teach Melba Lacy how to walk and stand and pronounce words properly. I feel like I am her guardian angel. I hope that is not sacrilegious! If it is I'll . . . what? The Jacksons don't go to church or pray or anything! I don't know why I think that's so bad because Mama and Daddy didn't go, either. If my dad walked into the church, it would probably explode in one big blast of sulphur.

Stop self! Stop! You cannot think of him!

I wonder if even God could save his soul.

That's not my problem! My calling in life is to help others!

I don't think I can help Dick or Frog, but Melba Lacy is like a sponge. She wants to learn everything, and no matter what she decides to do in her life, it will be a blessing to mankind.

Now if I can just figure out what I'm going to do with my life. . . .

Monday, October 11

I've become my teacher's helper. It isn't easy, but it's a powerful boost to my confidence. I now have thoughts that maybe someday I can be somebody . . . and that Melba Lacy can be an important somebody, too!

Wednesday, October 13

Life is not all bad! In fact, I suspect that Melba Lacy is teaching me to look for the good in life, in a way that I could never have done without her help.

Even in my classroom I'm noticing that nearly every time I say something nice and constructive to a pupil, they stand a little taller and sometimes smile even though it almost breaks their faces.

Monday, October 18

Today Mrs. Lakin, our teacher, was sick so we had a substitute. It was really sad, actually pathetic, because I was much more knowledgeable than she. How tragic it is that most . . . well probably not most . . . but many kids, like the kids in this school, never have a chance at a good teacher and a good education. That doesn't seem fair at all! But what can throw-away me do about it? Nothing!

Wait. That is not true! I can do something!

I've never been so grateful for the nuns teachings in my life. I can "do unto others as I would have them do unto me." I can know that love and caring and helping are among the greatest commandments given. I can serve others . . . not that I want to be a nun or something like that . . . and I can teach: honor, integrity, respect for self and others, the difference between right and wrong, courtesy, etc. I'll start with Melba Lacy, and then maybe go to Dick and Frog. I won't throw things into their faces; I'll just go quietly and lovingly beside them planting seeds. Sadly knowing that not all of the seeds will germinate.

Dear, precious Sister Mary explained to us once about our responsibility to, throughout our lives, plant seeds of beauty and love. That lecture didn't seem like much to me then, but now it seems like a holy commandment.

If I can take out some books from the school library, insignificant as it is, I can prepare Melba Lacy for a higher learning commitment! Maybe I can even encourage the boys, but I wouldn't bet my life on that.

Hey, wait a minute! What happened to my confidence and faith concept? I better start working on myself and that!

Wednesday, October 27

I can't believe how smart Melba Lacy is! When I first came here, I thought she was retarded. I really did! She went around being like Silly Suzy Sunshine and like the world was all peaches and cream, while I was mentally blaspheming every moment of my past life. Well, maybe I wasn't that bad, but I certainly wasn't doing much to pull myself out of the moral mud.

Actually I'm pretty proud of myself. Melba Lacy and I study every night for a couple of hours. She's learned how to pronounce words correctly, and she's becoming a pretty good reader. We read everything that's around: old newspapers, junk mail, but nothing from my journal. I don't want anyone in the whole world to ever know about it ever!

Dick and Frog are hopeless in the educational field. I hate to say this, but so are Mr. and Mrs. Jackson. We call them Mom and Dad when the Child Protection people come by, which isn't often, and we all hate the super-dumb questions they ask us. Like we'd dare tell them the truth . . . no way.

Actually the Jacksons aren't really that bad. I guess they do the best they know how. But truthfully they don't know much about anything, and don't care to learn. There are classes on TV that this whole family could learn from, but Mr. and Mrs. Jackson are always watching some idiotic program that just depletes their brains.

Not that I don't like television. I love it! It's just that Melba Lacy and I never get a chance to see anything we want.

Friday, October 29

I just noticed that I haven't written much about four-year-old Donita. I talked to Melba Lacy about Donita and we're going to start working with her. I really am almost sure that she has some mental deficiencies, but even if she does, we can help her become better than she is now. When I see how Melba Lacy is jumping forward in mathematics, I'm totally amazed. Every new concept to her is like receiving a fantastic present or a new game, and she appreciates it, while I always just took those things for granted. Maybe Donita will, too. . . . We wish . . .

Tomorrow Melba Lacy and I seriously start working with Donita. We've tried to hold her and love her, to take her for walks or brush her hair or scratch her back, but nothing works. We've got to find a new way . . . but we also have to be aware that she really might have, as Melba Lacy says, "a broken mind." I thought about that in the night and cried myself to sleep, but I am not going to give up!

Saturday, November 13

Melba Lacy and I have been working with Donita for weeks, but we haven't gotten anywhere! She still runs and hides under beds and behind chairs and stuff. It is really heartbreaking. Sometimes she even snarls at us, but without making a noise. We're both stumped!

I don't want Melba Lacy to get involved in this, but I think the next time the people come from Child Protection, I'm going to slip one of them a note asking if I can talk to someone about baby Donita. She certainly deserves something better than what she's getting here.

Surely there is someone, somewhere, who can help her! I'm praying for her with all my heart and so is Melba Lacy, since I've taught her to pray.

Monday, November 15

Every day I pray that the Child Protection people will come. It used to be that I hated having them come: asking us questions, giving us strange looks like they didn't believe a thing we said, and all kinds of other things that made us feel embarrassed and lowly. And unimportant! Will I always have to live here in this home of no future? Will dear little Donita and Melba Lacy? I want to pass a note to one of the welfare people, asking if I can talk to them alone about Donita. Surely they have some books or something that can help

Melba Lacy and me help baby Donita out of her almost animalistic behavior. Right now I feel that everyone in this house is totally imprisoned in a no-growth cycle!

Will the rest of our lives go on like this? Life sucks! Life really sucks! Life really, really sucks! Stop the world, I want to get off!

Wednesday, November 17

Every day is becoming more dreary. I'm helping others in school and at home but nobody is helping me. I know that sounds selfish and self-centered but it's true. How can I ever get out of this situation? How can I ever get an education? Without an education, how can I ever get a job? I don't want to be like the Jacksons! I don't want Melba Lacy and Donita to be like the Jacksons, either. I am so confused!

Friday, November 19

I'm getting so skinny that I have to use a big safety pin to keep my pants from falling off. Nothing tastes, or looks, or feels good. It's like I'm on automatic pilot.

When I first got here, Mrs. Jackson was doing some of the work around the house, but now she's as lazy as Mr. Jackson. They both sit and watch TV most of the day. Melba Lacy and I are expected to do all the cooking and cleaning and tending to Donita, etc. Not that there is much work in tending to her, she's like a little skinny shadow looking for a dark hole to hide in. Melba Lacy and I are trying our hardest to get her to let us hug her, or rock her, or even touch her. Most of the time she pulls away like we are trying to hurt her.

Saturday, November 20

Today it rained and Mr. Jackson put a big ladder up by the front window. Then he called Dick and Frog to go up and fix the leaks, which of course they didn't do!

Melba Lacy and I have been putting pans and buckets under all the leaky places, but we can't empty some of them fast enough. It's horrible. I wish I knew how to get in touch with the Child Protection people so I could at least report the problem. Once I looked behind a chair where there was a big leak, and there was little Donita with the dirty black water dripping down on her, and her looking like nothing unusual was happening. She always looks empty inside, like maybe there isn't a real person in there at all. It's scary!

Monday, November 22

The rain has finally stopped, but nobody has bothered to take down the ladder. Melba Lacy and I have been busy cleaning up the wet carpets and floors and stuff, including my bed. We tried to get it out of the way, but the room was too small, so I guess I'll sleep with Melba Lacy. It will be a tight squeeze in her cot. But at least we kept baby Donita's bed dry, not that she'd notice the difference. That was not nice to write! I love baby Donita with all my heart, and as much as I'd like to leave this dump, I can't even imagine being without Melba Lacy and Donita!

Thursday, November 25

The most horrible thing happened. It was just getting to be dusk when I felt so depressed I decided I'd climb up the ladder and sit on top of the house. I don't know why! I pulled myself up to the chimney and looked around the landscape. Everything looked green and clean, which made me feel a little better. Then I noticed some movement by the old chicken house. Dick and Frog were there with baby Donita . . . and for a second I couldn't believe what I saw. Dick had put her on the ground and was pulling down her pants. She was lying as still and quiet as a dead person.

I slid down the roof, almost missing the ladder, and ran toward Dick like an angry animal. Just before I got to him, I picked up a huge rock and smashed him on the head with it. He slumped down and I tried to hit him again but Frog stopped me. Blood was gushing out of Dick's head in all directions, much of it dripping on baby Donita. I kicked him aside and pulled Donita up. She was limp as a rag and her eyes looked totally blank.

I screamed at Dick that I wanted to kill him, and I certainly was going to notify the police. All the time I was hugging limp little Donita and rocking her back and forth. Frog put his hand over my mouth and told me they "weren't doin' nothin'." That infuriated me so much that I kicked him in the groin as hard as I could while still holding the baby. He screamed, then whimpered as he pulled Dick off the ground and the two of them hobbled off to Hades: the home of the dead beneath the earth! I savored that picture in my mind!

Donita didn't move a muscle as I carried her into the house. I cleaned her up and sat in the rocking chair snuggling her and petting her head. In a way, I hoped she *was* nearly brain-dead, because I didn't want her to have the awful reruns I often have rushing through my head, and probably always will have!

Friday, November 26

I sneaked a note into the principal's office box about Dick and Frog abusing baby Donita, but, of course, I didn't leave my name. I hope they are both caught and put into a juvenile detention place until they are old enough to go into a regular prison for forever!

1:35 a.m.

I woke up in the middle of the night having a nightmare of *my* horrific past experience. I wondered how many times poor little Donita had been abused. Only four years old and . . . I had to get up and throw up.

Thursday, December 16

It's been three weeks since the Donita thing. Dick and Frog have disappeared. The ladder is still leaning against the house. Mr. and Mrs. Jackson are still glued to their TV set. We haven't heard anything from the police or the Child Protection people. Each day each room in the house smells more moldy, and nothing has been done about the roof.

Monday, December 20

I'm worried about Donita's nutrition. According to what I learned in Sister Martha's health and nutrition class, mush and dried milk for breakfast, mashed potato sandwiches or plain bread sandwiches and water for lunch, and macaroni or beans for dinner aren't what one would call a good balanced diet. But what is there to do? There must be millions of kids who don't have the privilege of being wanted, or fed properly, or educated.

I'm getting thinner and more depressed every day!

Tuesday, January 4

Today I am on my way out of the dumps. Why? Because Donita smiled at me! It's the first time since I've been here that she's shown the slightest bit of interest in anything.

I was just sitting there rocking her, singing to her and patting her, after I'd cleaned up the breakfast things, and for one moment the veil lifted from her eyes and I knew that there was an important somebody inside that shell! It's a miracle! Just as I was going down for the third time in my own life . . . *Donita smiled*. Now I can't stop smiling myself.

I told Melba Lacy about the smile on the way to school, and she is as excited and delighted as I am. Somehow we're cracking open Donita's shell!

What a lovely, lovely day!

We're on our way!

Friday, January 7

The Child Protection people came today, and since I recognized their car coming down the road, I quickly scratched a little note about our bad food, and handed it to the lady as I opened the door. The ladies were shocked at the condition the house was in and immediately one of them pulled out her cell phone and reported the roof problem.

I was scared to death that I would get into trouble

for reporting the lack of nourishing food, but the lady I gave the note to was cool. She didn't even look at me when she told the Jacksons she was going to increase the money amount given to them so more could be spent on nourishing food.

After the Child Protection ladies left, Melba Lacy and I wondered if baby Donita would be better off in another home. She was alone all day with the Jacksons while we were in school, and we knew they gave her little, if any, care. But we cared! And she was, each day, acting a little more like a human being.

And what if they sent her to a place where she might be abused again? Wouldn't we forever and ever be guilty of that?

Maybe we better think on . . . whatever.

Monday, January 10

Today a girl at school gave me half of her cookie and I stuck it in my pocket to give to Donita. Not that I didn't want to eat it. I wanted to like everything! But I wanted even more to see Donita's face when she tasted the cookie.

By the time we'd had dinner (this time, thanks to the note, a decent dinner) and we'd straightened things up and got Mr. and Mrs. Jackson settled in front of the TV, it was nearly twilight.

Excitedly we sat on the porch steps and gave Donita

bits of cookie crumbs. With the first bite she looked like her old stoic self, with the second there was a tiny glow in her eyes, and with the third a beaming smile on her face! We were elated!

Melba Lacy took one hand and I took the other and we bounced Donita up and down the garden path. It was the first time that she had ever seemed like even a semi-real kid.

Laughing, we crumpled down on the ground and watched a few fireflies. Donita once even reached out like she wanted to touch one. Our hearts almost exploded with joy. Her mind wasn't blank. She wasn't an empty box!

Thursday, January 20

Every single day Donita is learning new things. She used to crawl more than she walked; now she loves taking walks with Melba Lacy and me, and she's beginning to talk a little, too. Her "Love you" doesn't sound much like "Love you," but she's trying and we're loving it. I know that there is no chance that she will pick up things like Melba Lacy, but she at least seems motivated to try, and maybe she can. I hope she can!

We haven't heard a thing about Dick and Frog. Maybe the Jacksons have, but they probably wouldn't have told us if they did know. I wish that I could wash the terrible thing with Donita out of my mind, but I guess it will live with me forever, like the other awful garbage that sometimes rolls around in my brain.

Tuesday, January 25

When I got home from school today, Donita was sitting on Mrs. Jackson's lap and Mrs. Jackson was rocking her and singing to her. I couldn't believe it! I'd always felt like the Jacksons were just kind of "wardens" for us who didn't care. Now I feel like they're probably doing the best they can with the education and background they've got. They, like us, at first thought Donita was just basically a body without a mind. It just shows how wrong all of us can sometimes be, and I'm really, really sorry about having felt that way.

Mr. Jackson is like a big, fat, lazy cat, sprawled out in his big chair, but he's never actually mean to any of us. I do appreciate being here with Melba Lacy and the precious new Donita who is beginning to unfold like a shining little miracle. She never hides under beds or behind chairs or in dark corners of closets anymore. She's our little sunbeam. Often Melba Lacy and I call her that. She sometimes even calls herself "Saabeam."

This is certainly a different world than the one I used to live in. In some ways it is better! At least we all know we're safe here, now that Dick and Frog have disappeared—into the underworld, we hope!

Sunday, January 30

I'm sitting out on the porch steps, writing in the moonlight. I hate to admit this but I miss a lot of things I used to have: the pool, the tennis court, Mrs. Jolettea, Cook, my wonderful old Catholic girls' school, the nuns (especially Sister Mary), my mama . . . *shh*— don't go there.

I've cried buckets of tears sitting here with the stars sprinkling down on me like even more tears. Actually, I think it's been therapeutic! I haven't been able to put Mama into a place in my heart where she belonged, until this very night. Often in the past, I've thought of her and her drug problem negatively. I'd felt that she was a wimp for not getting out of it, then tried to believe that she didn't really have a problem. Sometimes I blamed it on Daddy and sometimes on her weirder-than-weird doctor and her shadowy nurse. Now my heart breaks for her, and I think I'll call her from the school phone this very day. Just the thought of hearing her sweet loving voice gives me goose bumps. I know she's always loved me, she just didn't . . . I wish I knew how I could help her.

Monday, January 31

I'm completely fragmented! I called our old home number and it has been changed! Why would Daddy do that? Does he just want to hurt me more by hurting me through Mama? What if something has happened to her? She could be dead and I wouldn't even know it. I worried all day. Then, just before leaving school, I fearfully called Malie, Daddy's private secretary. I'd called her so often in the past that her number was filed in my brain.

Malie seemed glad to hear from me and wanted to know where I was and what I was doing. But of course I couldn't tell her, so I just hedged, saying my new school was really interesting and different . . . half lie . . . interesting? No. Different? In every way under the sun!

After a while Malie talked about Daddy's financial problems. I wanted her to mention Mama but she never did.

I hope Mama's happy there, but I can't wipe out the bad things Daddy (the stranger) said about her when . . . stop! You cannot allow yourself to think of those things! You've got to concentrate on your new family: Melba Lacy and Donita! You have got to teach both of them everything you have been taught!

Oh, please, please Jesus help me!

Tuesday, February 1

Melba Lacy and I have got to start praying for the Jacksons. I know they are doing the very best they know how, but it isn't much! That wasn't necessary! I know! And I'm going to be more considerate and appreciative of them. After all, I could be walking the street on Skid Row, or in Hollywood. Please, please Mind, don't ever let me think about that again!

Friday, February 4

I'm becoming depressed again. I'm fighting it like crazy, working my hardest at teaching Melba Lacy manners and social standards, working with her reading and math, begging for the privilege of taking home books from the library on subjects she will need if she ever gets the chance to go to a decent school. And at school I'm still my teacher's aide. Sometimes I think I work harder at teaching than she does. I'm also spending as much time as I can with Donita. She's coming along but she needs more assistance in more things than Mrs. Jackson can give her. I hate to say this, but love is not enough. Mrs. Jackson now rocks her and cuddles her as she watches television, but she isn't teaching her any of the skills she's going to need to become a well-rounded, successful person.

I feel so incompetent! I want to help everyone! And I can't even help myself. Each day I'm falling backward educationally. Will I ever be able to go to college? Wear nice clothes? Associate with people who are intellectuals? Do some little something to make the world a better place? If it weren't for Donita and Melba

Lacy I'd just want to go to bed, go to sleep, and never wake up!

Monday, February 7

I know I'm still, for some unknown reason, losing weight, but it really hurt my feelings today when Ruppert, in front of the whole class, called me Bony-Butt Katie. I pretended I didn't care, but I do! I want to be somebody, and I can't see a possible way to make that happen.

I'm trying my hardest to be positive and helpful, but each day it seems like I'm sinking deeper and deeper into the cold black earth.

Melba Lacy is doing so well in school and socially that I'm proud of her to my very bones. And dear, precious little Donita is the light of my life! I'm teaching her to enunciate instead of garble, and she is totally amazing. We play games with sounds and then we, in our own silly way, make them into words, then short sentences. Today she is saying, "Donita is happy." To everything she sees; birds, flowers, people, and especially the doll the Child Protection lady gave her the last time she was here. She's also standing straight and tall now, not like a string of wet spaghetti.

It's amazing what a few months and lots and lots of loving teaching can do to change an almost-vegetable into a cheerful, trusting child. Often when I'm rocking her and singing to her I feel almost like she is my child. And at times, like now, I think maybe she is the only thing that keeps me afloat.

Wednesday, February 23

Mrs. Jackson fell down the basement steps a couple of weeks ago and hurt her back. Since then I've also taken on the "mother" role. It's too bad that her accident happened just as she was kind of beginning to understand a little about what "mothering" is! I remember when we went through the mothering section in a mental health class. Sister Martha would have made a wonderful mother. I wonder why she became a nun.

Lately I'm often getting so weary that I wonder if a convent isn't where I'm going to wind up.

Tuesday, March 1

Today the Child Protection ladies came again. They were absolutely amazed by the change in Donita, her running around and talking and laughing. She even sang a little song for them, which Melba Lacy and I had made up:

I'm happy, you're happy, happy is nice.
I'm happy, you're happy. . . .
Sing the song twice.

We all laughed and clapped our hands after she had finished, and Miss Martin reached into her purse and found a piece of candy for Donita. Little Donita was so excited she wanted each of us to take a lick.

Our little ugly duckling has turned into a beautiful miniature princess! The frightened child who had, not long ago, shrunk away from every living thing now belongs to the happy side of life! My heart thumped with joy.

By the time Miss Martin had finished with her Child Protection checklist, she too had fallen in love with the sunshiny little creature who used to be just a blob.

Thursday, March 3

Miss Witterhouse, who teaches fifth grade and is also the school nurse, saw me leaning against the hall wall and suggested I come into the First Aid Room. I tried to perk up and follow her, but even walking was hard. She asked me lots of questions and took my blood pressure and stuff, then asked me what I was eating and doing during school and at home. I told her what I thought she wanted to hear, just as the bell rang.

On the way home on the bus Melba Lacy said Miss Witterhouse had asked her into the First Aid Room and had quizzed her in detail about me. I felt uncomfortable as she said she had told the absolute truth about me doing most of the work around the house, as well as tutoring her about everything important to get into college, so she could get a good job and be a somebody! She also told Miss Witterhouse that I was basically the one who had gotten through Donita's hard shell and into her heart and a lot of other stuff that she had a big part in! I reached over and hugged her for making me seem so magnanimous. I'd always wanted to have that word bestowed upon me, since the day I first heard it in a spelling bee study.

Goodnight dear little sisters, Donita and Melba Lacy.

I rarely think of Dick and Frog anymore, or my stranger daddy and what's happened to Mama. What will happen to her when she's no longer young and beautiful? But I can't allow myself to think about that. It's too painful. Painful is not nearly a destructive enough word!

Friday, March 4

Miss Witterhouse met me in the hall at lunchtime and gave me some vitamins and minerals to take. She also said I'd been working too hard, both at school as a teacher's aide and in the mother role since Mrs. Jackson had been "laid up out of commission."

Uggggh, I'm beginning to understand their slovenly verbalizations.

But that doesn't make me better than they are, especially after Daddy, who I trusted implicitly . . . don't go there self! Go to sleep and dream sweet dreams of the glorious future that Melba Lacy and Donita and you are headed for.

Saturday, March 5

Last night on the porch steps, Melba Lacy and I talked about everything good that was going to happen in our lives. How we were going to go to college on scholarships. (How I'm going to manage that is left up to faith at this moment.)

I don't know what happened to Melba Lacy, but while we were looking up at the stars, talking about how beautiful they were, she quietly said, "I'm going to change my name to Star." It took me a long time to explain how hard it would be to legally change her name.

Melba Lacy (who usually spreads sunshine around every thing she touches) seemed so downcast that I tried to raise her spirits, but I couldn't, not one bit.

Finally she snuggled close to me and whispered that she hated the name Melba because it was also her mother's name, and that she had let him do the bad things to her.

Tears overwhelmed me as they froze into hard rocks of ice throughout my body. This priceless little girl who had chosen to be a friend and neighbor to everyone she met had herself been abused. Still she had somehow turned the anger into love, at least for most people.

We wept together and clung terrified in a black limbo, until I was able to tell her a little about my time when . . .

She pulled away from me in the middle of my first sentence and crumpled against the porch post. Then she told me that her father had hurt her as far back as she could remember, often with her mother passed out at his side.

By that time I was numb. Still I slowly slid toward her. "You're right, little sister," I whispered. Then I told her I thought we should take her name "Melba" and go bury it behind the chicken pen, never to even think of it again.

She agreed and we wrapped the name Melba in an old piece of newspaper, placed it deep in the ground, and covered it with chicken droppings. Then we crossed our hearts and repeated our vow not to ever, ever, ever think of our . . . bad things . . . again.

When we got back to the middle of the yard, a lacy trail of white cloud floated over and between the stars, almost in a blessing kind of way! "See those lacy white clouds? They have chosen your new name," I whispered as I hugged her so hard she gasped. "The name Melba that was your mother's is gone, and now there's only you, Lacy."

"Lacy, Lacy, Lacy . . . " she repeated over and over,

as though she had never heard the word before.

It was very late when we started for the house! But we had dumped mounds of mental garbage. I felt a lot like the new Lacy, that I had buried a lot of my mental garbage, too.

Monday, March 7

I think my vitamins, minerals, and strict eating patterns are doing me good. Miss Martin from Child Protection makes sure we get the right food every week now, but Mrs. Jackson is still unable to do any work around the house.

Lacy and I found some old rope and made a swing for Donita. She loves it and sings:

> Up, up in the sky,
> Where the little birds fly
> With Donita and Lacy and Katie.

It's funny how nobody seemed to have any kind of problem with Lacy's name, not even the kids at school.

Tuesday, March 8

Often I dream about Mark and Jennifer and the dear, dear nuns that sometimes I used to think were too strict. How grateful I am for the wonderful education they gave me, and that I can share at least some of it with Lacy. Sometimes I literally cry over the lazy way the kids are taught here. Education isn't thought of as one of "the majestic stairways to eternity," as Sister Mary used to call it. I wish, I wish, I wish I could go back! But that would only be if I could take Lacy and Donita with me! They are now my family, and I must prepare them to get out of this lower-class existence! In many ways they aren't even aware of what wonderful things are going on outside this rural little community. If they only knew about museums, with dinosaurs and statues and things that existed long, long before the time of Jesus . . . and aquariums, and the Hollywood Bowl, and planetariums, and just walking through great universities, like UCLA, and seeing thousands and thousands of books, all in good condition, in the libraries. There are so many things I want to teach them and show them!

Wednesday, March 9

Today has been the blackest day of my life!

The Child Protection ladies came and Miss Martin, without any warning, told us that she had found a wonderful home for Donita, "now that she had come out of her shell and is becoming, in all ways, like a normal child."

I don't know how Miss Martin could have prepared

us for this, and I guess I should be happy that Donita is going to a nice home in Pasadena, which is a lovely city, but still it's like tearing out and taking away part of my heart.

I could tell by the look on Lacy's face, and the tears in her eyes, that she feels exactly like I do.

The ladies and Mrs. Jackson started talking about some papers and saying it was hard to put black children into prestigious homes. That Donita would be lucky!

I wanted to scream and tell them how "lucky" I was! Prestigious home? Yes! Loving and caring home? No. My nannies and tutors, especially the nuns, taught me everything I know about the good and right things in life. What if the new family isn't good to Donita?

Miss Martin had lured Donita up onto her lap with some Hershey's Kisses. Lacy and I watched as she reached into her bag for toys to play with and cookies to munch on. With broken hearts we knew that she had been bought and paid for by the system.

Something inside tried to tell me that maybe Donita would be going to a wonderful home, with love, music, and laughter filling in every room. Maybe I was just being possessive and jealous because I had been mainly the one who dragged Donita out of her black, closed-out pit, inch by inch, syllable by syllable, musical note by musical note, touch by touch, hug by hug! I wanted what was best for her! I did! I do! I really do! But at the same time I feel like I'm losing a part of myself.

Donita kissed Lacy and me before she, with an armful of presents, skipped, humming and happy, to the car that was going to take her to another life.

After the car had disappeared out of sight, Mrs. Jackson sat down on the steps with Lacy and me and we all cried for a while. Then Mrs. Jackson told us what she said she shouldn't tell us.

It seems some different ladies, who had brought Donita to her house, had left a stack of papers on her table. Papers that told about her past: horrible, almost unspeakable, sexual, physical, and verbal abuse. When the Jacksons got her she was like a rag doll. She could not walk, talk, or feed herself, and at times she seemed almost blind, her eyes were so unfocused.

Mrs. Jackson credited me entirely with bringing the child out of her shell. That wasn't really true because Lacy helped a lot. Little Lacy who sees only the good in life. She seems to be able to overlook, or something, the old bad things in her life while I seem to be hanging onto mine like I will never let go! I wish I could let go . . .

Dear, dear Jesus, please, please help me to let go.

Thursday, March 10

Lacy and I both cried and prayed for Donita most of the night. Twice Lacy sneaked to my cot and we cuddled together and whispered about dear little Donita, and how hard it would be to live here without her.

This morning Lacy and I asked Mrs. Jackson if we could possibly phone Donita or write to her. Mrs. Jackson said there was no way we could do that.

All day at school I was like a zombie, worrying about Donita, wanting to go and kidnap her and Lacy and take them . . . where? Lacy had been in three different homes before she came here. I don't know if they moved her around because . . . Oh, I hope not! But why would they move her if . . . maybe the people got sick . . . or died . . . or . . .

Monday, March 14

Today is another hellish one. The Child Protection ladies, this time a different pair, brought Charles and Belva to become part of our family. Both of them seemed sullen and angry. When they were introduced to us Charles whispered, while the ladies were talking, "You hos call me Charles and I'll scramble your brains. My name is Cha!" The look on his face made us think he really meant what he said, and that we will call him Cha forever more.

Tuesday, March 15

Lacy and I have been sitting out on the steps talking for hours, wondering if Donita is missing us as much as we are missing her, wondering if she'll have a mother or a nanny who will encourage her to grow mentally and in every other way.

We pretended that she now lives in a lovely little cottage with a swimming pool and a nice clean room of her own, and a mother who spoils her terribly . . . not really spoils her, but teaches her to find happiness by doing unto others as she would have them do unto her. That is what dear Lacy does, and she didn't even know she was doing it until I told her about the nuns.

As much as I miss Donita, which is with every cell in my body, I'm glad she isn't here. I don't trust Cha one bit, and I wouldn't be surprised if he . . . Oh, come on Katie, now you are conjuring up trouble.

Wednesday, March 16

When Dick and Frog were here, they slept in the same room. Now Belva has the extra cot in with us. It is so crowded we almost have to hop over each other, and we can't whisper to each other any time we want because Belva curses at us and tells us to "Shut the —— up." She has got the worst dirty mouth I've ever heard.

In fact, half of her vocabulary I don't even understand. It's almost like a foreign language . . . but you can still tell it's obscene!

Thursday, March 31

I'm worried about Lacy. Cha and Belva are always buying her stuff and giving her money, and they are keeping her away from me as much as they can. They always sit with her between them on the bus, and they are nice to her while they ignore me completely. I hope they aren't going to pull her away from me.

Lacy has been doing so well in all the different categories of life that my self-confidence hasn't been in the dumps all the way. She's been helping her teacher and getting fantastic grades on all her tests. But for some unknown reason she's still being pulled toward Cha and Belva like a magnet. In our cramped surroundings at home or on the bus, I haven't been able to talk to her without having Cha or Belva over my shoulder.

Something is going on that is making goose bumps hop up and down my back!.

I know that Lacy isn't working on her homework like she used to and that I'm seeing money change hands in a way that is really suspicious. But I can't find a way to talk to Lacy about it. No telling what Cha and probably Belva would do to me, or Lacy, if I tried to get in their way. They are really sweet to both Mr. and Mrs. Jackson at home. I know it's fake but obviously the Jacksons don't!

Sometimes on the school grounds Cha and Belva are like demonic animals. And once on the bus, I saw Cha take a small knife out of his pocket and stab a kid in the arm because he wouldn't change seats with him. Then he whispered something to the kid that made his face turn white and he immediately got up and moved.

I'm scared of Cha and Belva twenty-four hours a day, because they are estranging Lacy from me, but mainly because they are leading her astray and I can't understand how they are doing that! I'm so worried I can't sleep, I'm beginning to get depressed again, and I constantly dream about little Donita. Life is . . . I'm not even going to write it!

Thursday, April 7

Today Cha and Belva didn't get on the bus after school. After we'd gone a few blocks Lacy came over and sat by me. We wondered what had happened to them. When we got home Mrs. Jackson was furiously out of control. She said the school had called and Cha and Belva had been picked up for selling drugs on the school grounds. Then she yelled and swore about how hard it was to have delinquent, evil kids in your home. She acted like we were as bad as they were and we crept outside to get out of her way.

All during dinner Mrs. Jackson complained about how hard she had it and how nobody appreciated everything she did for them, and who in hell she'd get to take Cha's and Belva's places. We were glad when the Jacksons got through slurping down their food and waddled in to the living room to become one with their television programs.

Friday, April 8

Sitting on the porch steps and listening to the crickets and watching the moon and stars (that is, when you can see them through the smog) is therapeutic.

For two or three weeks, Lacy has been in the grip of Cha and Belva. Poor little naïve thing! She really thought they were doing good. They had told her that a wealthy man Cha knew was giving him money to give to throw-away kids like us. She wanted to give some to me, but Cha said I had disrespected him and she had to choose between helping poor kids or doing my selfish thing. She started crying then like the dam within her had broken and I held her tight and told her over and over that she hadn't done anything wrong.

After a few minutes of blubbering and sniffing, she told me how she had given kids little envelopes Cha said were full of money to help them buy things they could in no other way have. They, in turn, gave her back little envelopes to give to Cha and Belva.

She broke down completely then, and put her head in my lap, sobbing that she was as bad as they were . . . and she would probably go to jail with them . . . that she deserved it for being so gullible. She asked me if I could ever forgive her and if I would come and visit her in the juvenile hall. We were like real sisters again, clinging together like we had no one, or nothing, to cling to!

Sunday, April 10

For three days Lacy and I have both been thinking that at any moment the police would drive up to the door, or the phone would ring, wanting Lacy to come to juvenile court or something. We were being like angels, cleaning up the house after we'd made breakfast, mowing the lawn, trimming the hedges, fixing dinner, and cleaning up. Being so polite and grateful for just being together that we could hardly stand it.

Lacy couldn't believe that she had literally been selling drugs. She, the Pollyanna of all Pollyannas, being a schoolyard pusher.

During the night she sneaked over and scrunched up beside me on my tiny cot. She was sure Cha and Belva would tell everybody everything . . . and more . . . like she really knew what she was doing. All I could do was hug her and over and over again saying

"*Shhhhhhhhh, shhhhh, shhhhhhhhhhhhh*. God is in His heaven, all is right with the world."

I don't know where I read that or heard it, but it made us feel better and we did fall asleep.

Friday, May 6

It's been a month since the Cha and Belva thing and no one has come to put handcuffs on Lacy, or anything like that. So we're feeling fairly safe, except that Lacy has lost all of her self-confidence! She used to be Little Miss Sunshine, always trying to make others comfortable and happy. Now it's like a little black cloud is hanging over her.

Oh, and a few days ago the Child Protection ladies brought in two truly sad-looking girls. They had been picked up trying to hitchhike to Bakersfield. Both of them are really fat and stringy-haired, and Lacy and I don't think Mr. and Mrs. Jackson like them very much.

We're trying to be extra nice to them, teaching them how to set the table and make beds and . . . I couldn't believe that they were so unskilled and uneducated. Lacy once giggled that they must have been raised in a barn. Then she reverted back to her old self and said we must do everything we can to help them out of their black pit. We looked at each other and knew it was dreadful, without either one of them even mentioning it!

Wednesday, May 11

Lacy is her old self again. Helping Minnie and Sara with every detail in their lives, adoring her teacher and helping her with papers and things like that. I'm about back to my old self, too, and really trying to make our home, humble as it is, livable. Also I've made a commitment to myself that I will teach Minnie and Sara to be refined young ladies. Well . . . maybe not in all ways refined, but at least I will teach them to bathe regularly, to brush their teeth, to wash their hair, and the joy of studying and learning etc.!

Thursday, May 12

I wrote that Lacy is her old self again, but actually she is a completely new self! Miss Lakin, my teacher, asked me to take some things into Lacy's classroom and when I got there and saw how efficient and confidence-inspiring she was, I wanted to tell everyone there that she is my sister!

After class I hurried back to Lacy's room and told her teacher how wonderful Lacy was and how proud of her I was! The teacher laughed and said, "I guess I've been taking her for granted," she paused, ". . . and when I think about it, I don't know how I could teach without her."

That made me feel so good I was skipping inside myself for the rest of the day.

Friday, May 13

It seems like I've been here forever, trying to help everybody and everything like Sister Mary taught me to do, but who is trying to help me? I'm not progressing, advancing, moving onward and upward. I can't think of one thing I've learned, and I want to graduate from high school with some honors and go on to college! I must! That has always been my dream. Not the nightmare I'm now in . . . where I'll probably be forever.

Black, Black Tuesday, May 24

Lacy's teacher ran into me in the hall and enthusiastically asked me to meet her at lunchtime. She had brought a bag lunch, and we sat out on the old rusty bench by the front door. She shared her sandwich. Then she told me how much she admired Lacy and the wonderful things she was doing for some of the other pupils. She said she had never had a student so willing to learn and so eager to help. Then she shared a secret with me that I promised not to repeat: She had been invited to be a vice-principal at a really nice school in Culver City, and she wanted to take Lacy with her. Her aunt, who lived in Culver City, had taken in foster children at one time, and when she heard about Lacy, "the totally unusual child," she thought she'd love having her. She had been a teacher herself at one time, and felt it would be a wonderful experience for the two of them, even though now she was too old to take foster children by herself.

With all my heart I wanted to go with Lacy! The aunt had a cozy little cottage within walking distance of what would be their school. And it was a good school, not like this dumpy one. I could see that Lacy's teacher was reading my mind by the sad look on her face, and I could tell that the aunt didn't want two children.

Life is not kind.

Sunday, June 5

I've had the flu or something all the time Lacy was getting ready to leave; throwing up and having diarrhea and headaches, as well as a heartache, that has me doubled over in cramps. I want to die! I want to go back to Mama and Daddy. Probably by now Mama's kicked her problem and Daddy has kicked his. Oh please, Jesus, why have you forsaken me?

Tuesday, June 14

I'm back in school but I'm not well. I do everything that has to be done around the house and in class, but I am always so tired . . . so I-want-to-lie-down-and-never-ever-get-up. I hope I don't have cancer or something. Maybe I do; it's got to be something awful. I feel lonely and scared and unwanted. I remember once when I was little, one of the kids in the playground started saying, "Nobody loves me, everybody hates me, I'm going out to eat worms." I don't know why that popped into my mind but maybe it's because it is true; nobody does like me. Everybody does hate me . . . but I'm not sure about the "worms" part.

Saturday, August 6

Mrs. Jackson still isn't well and had to be taken to the hospital. The Child Protection ladies came and took Minnie and Sara and me to a house with six kids in it. It's a scary place. All of them, including me, are sort of semi-people, at least relative to the girls in the Catholic girls' school.

I'm trying to be positive and friendly, but I can't quite get up the energy to make it happen. It's like I'm walking through mud up to my knees, maybe up to my chin. I don't belong anywhere . . . and I want to belong!

My mind is tumbling with fears about little Donita and Lacy. Maybe not Lacy, because I know she's got a good, loving home. I envy her! I truly with all my heart envy her! I know that is wrong, but I can't help it!

I guess I shouldn't be feeling so bad because Joanne, whose bed is next to mine, has been in six different homes since she was taken away from her parents. What a desperate way to exist. I wonder if it's harder for me because I once lived in almost a fairytale existence? Probably not, even though I've got wonderful, wonderful things to think about. If only I could shut out the bad things that seem to always be roaring around in my brain.

Tuesday, August 16

Joanne seems much like me, sort of quiet and scared to the bone. I thought it was strange at first that she always wore shirts or blouses with long sleeves and long pants. Then one day I saw her getting dressed and she had a lot of red scars. I'd seen them on baby Donita and knew immediately that they were cigarette burns. I wanted to cry my head off, but I didn't, I just waited until we had a chance to be together outside and we talked about our problems. Talking is good! I learned that from Jason, who picked me up from the dark, evil, Los Angeles Skid Row streets and took me to the Salvation Army shelter. Dear, dear Jason, what ever would have happened to me without him?

Tuesday, September 6

The teachers at our new school are not as much teachers as they are babysitters, just trying to keep the kids halfway quiet and in their seats. I'm getting depressed again because I can't see that I've learned a single thing in the year that I've been in the system. In fact, I feel like much that I'd learned before I got into the system has been drained out of me, that I'm getting more stupid each day instead of more knowledgeable! That is pathetic and sad, but something deep inside tells me it's true.

I used to think I hated the strict discipline they had in my Catholic school, but now I suspect that would do wonders for schools like this.

I try not to, but I usually cry myself to sleep wishing I had Donita and Lacy, and . . . Mama and Daddy . . . he wasn't all bad . . . and she wasn't well . . .

> *If only . . .*
> *I'm lonely.*
> *I'm scared.*
> *And I'm sad.*
> *It must be because*
> *I'm bad.*
> *Nobody wants me.*
> *Nobody cares.*
> *Nobody cares.*
> *Nobody cares.*

Wednesday, September 7

Sometime during the night it seemed to me that Sister Mary came and whispered in my ear that the only way to be happy is to help others. Then she told me how much she missed me in school and how I was needed! And that great things were in store for me.

I could almost feel her and smell her sweet kind of spearmint breath and I couldn't wait for morning so I could talk to Joanne.

I was needed! Great things were in store for me! The concept was so uplifting that I knew I would never again in my life feel that I was the dregs of the earth.

Sad times? Maybe. Hurtful times? Probably! Happy times? Positively! And I suspected I would have to make many of the happy times for myself. But I can do that! And with God's help, I will!

For a while there I had about given up on everything! Now! Glory Hallelujah!

Joanne, aren't you ever going to wake up?!

I'm going to teach you everything I know like I did with Lacy, Lacy, Lacy! My friend, my sister, who I know I will someday meet again. Through the Culver City school I will find her. . . . Hopefully in time, I will be able to contact Donita, too. I pray they are happy and loved.

I feel that they are and that makes me feel loved, too!

Thursday, September 8

Joanne is going to need a lot of help! She's eleven years old, but she reads at about a second-grade level.

Her grammar is atrocious and her manners are non-existent. Poor little kid didn't even know how to use a toothbrush. Still she is so gentle and sweet that I sometimes call her "Sugar." I told her how I'd once seen a movie and the mom had called her little girl "Sugar." We both laughed about that and kept it as our own secret.

Tuesday, September 20

I'm finding it totally amazing that I at first thought that Lacy and Donita, and now Joanne, were all slightly retarded. Then when I started teaching them one on one, I found that they were all starving for knowledge! It's like it's a happy, exciting, challenging game that they can't play often enough. I'm so proud of them. I just hope they will all be allowed to continue having good, caring teachers to bless their lives, no matter where they are.

I just had a very frightening thought. Is it possible that most of the kids who seem so dumb at the schools I've been to since I left the private Catholic school just lack one-on-one teachers? Or maybe disciplined, yet caring, consistent guidance and training? I suspect most, if not all, of them need ego boosting and complimenting, instead of the ugliness and evilness that took them away from their homes in the first place. I wonder if anyone who has not been abused can even conceive of the permanent scars abuse leaves.

Come on self! Whining doesn't heal anything. Hard work and faith does!

Life is hard but it's still good! Now I'm being Pollyanna Lacy, and I love it!

Just thinking of Lacy brings up my spirits. Maybe that is what is wrong with the world. Not enough Pollyannas (excessively or persistently optimistic persons).

Oh, that there were more of them, and I was always one of them!

Monday, September 26

Joanne is perhaps the brightest kid I've ever seen! When I first met her, she was so shy and mentally and physically uncoordinated that I really did think she was somewhat mentally impaired. However, after I began telling her how much potential she had locked up inside herself, she started to slowly and cautiously open up like a flower in the sun.

I recited a little poem I'd learned from the nuns.

You can if you try,
and then by and by
you'll get to the top
and you never will stop.
As days pass along

you will always stay strong.
Look for love in mankind
and that's just what you'll find.

Joanne giggled and then repeated the poem slowly and perfectly. That was a blow to my ego because I'd had to read it a few times before I memorized it. I asked her if she'd learned it someplace else and she said, "No." Hmmmmmmmm . . .

Joanne's memory was great, but her spelling, reading, and math were way below normal. As we worked together, I found out that she didn't even know what the word *phonics* was. Nor did she understand numbers.

Every evening after the dinner table is cleaned up, Joanne and I study. I don't have any material that will expand my mind, but at least I can help her expand hers. She is unbelievably bright once she gets the hang of things, and her retention is amazing, even awesome!

Friday, October 14

Joanne and I have been working very seriously for the past five weeks trying to work up to her grade-age level. It's like I am her personal tutor. There are still many things I can teach her but she's getting a little bored, and a couple of the guys are trying to sneak up on her. I'm not going to teach her any more about posture and hair styles, etc. She's too vulnerable.

What can I do to intrigue her with something positive, something fascinating that will stimulate her brain instead of her hormones? Hormones are a big problem in foster homes.

Saturday, October 15

I couldn't sleep last night I was so worried about Joanne. I tried to think of something. I racked my brain, but nothing came up. As a last resort, I prayed and prayed. Still nothing.

I woke up just as the gray dawn was beginning to take over the darkness, and since I didn't have anything else to do, I started writing. After a minute or two I heard and felt Joanne squirming on the top bunk.

She leaned her head over the bed and whispered, "Are you awake?"

"Yeah." I whispered back. "Did I wake you up?"

She crept down into my bunk and clung to me, sniffling softly, "I'm so bored and left out and empty," she put her head in her hands and tried not to cry loud enough to wake up the two girls in the beds opposite us. "I don't want to drink with the guys and take drugs and . . . you know, but . . . life is such a bore . . . a drag . . . it's dull and boring and dumb!"

After a minute or two she looked at me pleadingly

and asked what I did to grow instead of wilt!

I reached over to push my papers away and she looked like the newborn sun was shining right out of her face. "I know!" she mouthed. "You write."

At first I didn't want to let her read my stuff. It was filled with too much evil and degradation. Then I realized that she had, I was almost sure, painful torments of her own to reckon with.

With some trepidation, we crept into the living room and she began poring over my papers, reading and weeping, then reading and weeping some more. It was hurtful as anything to both of us, but cathartic at the same time.

Wednesday, November 2

After that night Joanne lost all interest in the boys that had been trying to seduce her into their lifestyle. She again became fascinated with seeing, in her future, all the things she had only dreamed about in her past.

For the next few weeks, Joanne took advantage of every chance she had at school, which weren't many. I tutored her at home, and she accepted every suggestion I gave her as a gift. Each night she wrote religiously on the backs of the principal's throw-away papers. I never asked her, but I hoped someday she would let me read her journal.

This evening Joanne handed me her journal and begged me not to hate and despise her because . . .

Joanne told me her story.

Joanne's mother, Martha, was fifteen when she got pregnant with her. Joanne's grandmother disowned both of them, and Joanne was born in a junkie's bed. Her father could have been anyone on the street.

Joanne was placed in the foster care system and had undergone and tolerated five different placements by the time she was eight.

I couldn't stop crying when Joanne told me that things got worse after that.

Joanne wrote that at one time she lived in a trailer with nine other kids. The four smallest ones slept foot to foot, two in a bunk. The foster parents abused them, both physically and verbally. Joanne showed me a scar on the right side of her head where her foster mother had hit her with a hammer.

When Joanne was ten, the foster care system sent Joanne back to live with her grandmother, who had a scroungy boyfriend who tried to "do" her whenever her grandmother's head was turned. Joanne was glad when someone shot his face off in front of their house, and he died screaming. Joanne said she couldn't stop laughing for some crazy irrational reason, and her grandma kept slapping her until the police came and took away both the bloody boyfriend and her.

Joanne wrote that at the next foster home she stayed in, if anyone wet the bed they slept in it, if they had to throw up before they got outside, they had their face pushed into it, then they cleaned it up, no matter how sick they were. If they didn't do exactly what the foster parents wanted . . . Joanne put her face in her hands and sobbingly whispered, "You don't want to know what they did!"

I held her tightly in my arms and didn't want to ever let her go, with part of my heart knowing that any day we could be torn apart, never to see each other again.

I was furious. Over and over I asked how and why they could get away with those things.

Joanne winced, shrugged her shoulders, and said that foster parents get so many hundreds of dollars each month to take care of kids, and that they get even more if they take in kids with physical, mental, or social disabilities.

Thursday, November 3

At first, I had a hard time forcing myself to read about Joanne's past. Then one day I saw how much good it was doing her to sort of regurgitate the inhumanity of mankind. Sometimes she cried as she wrote, other times she swore or rammed her hands into a pillow or a chair, on occasion scraping off her skin.

Later I noticed something strange. The more she wrote about her problems and hurts and fears, the less angry she appeared. Actually it was like, even though her life had been hurtful and sometimes horrible, she was now becoming stronger because of it! Stronger and more compassionate and considerate of those around her who also had been, or now were, suffering.

I admired her so much I wanted to give her a Purple Heart or something! Of course I couldn't do that, so I gigglingly gave her a big hug!

The girls who slept in the bunks across from us happened to come in just then, and they couldn't wait to spread the lying word around that we were "queers," doing "it" on my bed in front of everybody. We heard that somebody said we even let people watch if they paid us. How disgusting can that be? How humiliated can we be?

We are the laughingstock and the butt of every imaginable dirty joke, not only in the trailer but also at school.

The teachers tried to pretend they weren't hearing what the kids said, but we knew they were! It was horrendous, vulgar, and obscene! I felt sorry for myself, but even worse for Joanne, because she is so much younger than I am, and so much more vulnerable!

I wanted to wait until the middle of the night and then run away with Joanne. But run where? I felt completely useless. It hurt so much that I, who was trying to be sweet little Joanne's mentor . . . maybe even her mother . . . was being comforted and taken care of by her!

Thank goodness for tears that help wash away at least some of the degradation and pain.

The two of us have seen more depravity in our lives, and lack of care, than we dared think about. I probably had seen and experienced much less than a lot of the kids. Kids probably by the hundreds . . . no thousands . . . maybe millions . . . who have lived parts of their lives in situations that no sane adult would want to know about, or think about, or do anything about! Kids, even baby kids, like Donita, are sexually abused from the time they are almost newly born. Is it because sexual abuse to a child seems too improbable and impossible for an adult to . . . who knows?

And other abuse: mental, physical, verbal? Like teenage kids having to wear diapers and no pants all of Saturday and Sunday if they wet their bed or did anything else the foster parents disliked. Joanne said she once had to lick up her own vomit, and another time she was not allowed food or water from Friday till Monday after school. She was so weak she passed out for a while on the bus. But no one dared tell because then they might find themselves in a worse situation.

Living in a foster home is almost like living in a

horror movie. No! That isn't right! Some of the people do the best they can. But others do unthinkable, brutal things. Joanne and I talk about the situation often.

Friday, November 4

In the middle of the night, Joanne crept down into my bunk and we decided that we were going to make a difference! We were going to cut school and go to the police station to tell our story, then to our small town newspaper and the school principal. Joanne is more responsible for the idea than I, and I am proud of her.

She said she had stayed awake all night thinking that without my positive help and teaching she might very easily have become one of the angry, unhinged kids who were trying so hard to demean us. She asked, "How would I have known wrong from right, good from bad, if you hadn't taught me?" She said she and Donita and Lacy all owed their lives to me, no matter where they now were.

Saturday, November 5

We got up, quickly and quietly dressed, then sneaked out into the cold night (almost morning) air, trying to get our act together. It was scary! What if . . . ?

But we chickened out! Halfway to the police station we were almost sure that the police wouldn't believe us and that none of the other kids would dare tell the truth and be on our side. Besides, ours was one of the better foster homes, and Joanne and I would surely be separated so we wouldn't cause any more problems. We decided that even the possibility of separation was too great a price to pay right now. But down the road, sooner or later, we will get up the guts to do something . . . I hope!

Monday, November 7

At school today I heard someone crying in the girls bathroom. Since there was no one else in there, I knocked on her stall and asked if there was anything I could do to help. She sobbed for another minute, then came out and said she was crying because . . . maybe . . . she was going to be adopted. I guess she saw the puzzled look on my face because she wiped her eyes with a piece of toilet paper and blew her nose, then said she was crying for happiness.

Other girls were coming in, so the two of us walked out into the hall, then down to the lunchroom where we found a semi-quiet place in a corner. There she told me about how she had wanted to be adopted her whole life.

Almost like we were close friends, she told me about her sickening background and how the police had come to her house during a terrible drunken fight between her mother and father and she had been dragged away. She'd been about four or five years old and had thought the policemen, with their guns out, were the bad people. They took her and her brother, Seth, just a little younger than she was, to a scary, noisy place, separated them, and she hadn't seen or heard from Seth since. She longed for her brother and worried about him for the next four years while she moved from foster home to foster home.

Now she might truly be going to a "real home." The family had seen pictures of her and a report on her and she had seen pictures of the people who wanted her. She said that with such joy in her voice that I thought she would probably die if they changed their minds. She talked a lot about how mean and cruel her parents had been when they were drinking, and how, in spite of that, she deeply yearned for them, or anyone else who would, or could, fill up the big empty hole in her life.

The bell rang and we all scurried off to our classes, and only then did I realize that I didn't even know the girl's name. She was just another foster kid nobody! But soon, I hoped, she would be adopted by a nice family with a pretty home, with people who would love her and be good to her. And maybe someday she would meet her little brother, Seth, like I dreamed of someday meeting Donita and Lacy.

After the two evil, lying, bad-mouthed witches in their bunks across from us were asleep. I told Joanne all about the girl with no name who might soon be adopted. Joanne sighed, then cried, and told me how much she had always wanted to be adopted. Me? I don't know. I'm afraid my trust mechanism is still so far out of whack that . . . Still, living in a loving family . . .

I think I'm too old to be adopted. I'm sure most people would want sweet little tiny tots. I can't allow myself to think about it. It is too painful! All I can hope for, at this point, is that I can get a good education . . . but that will take a miracle and a half! And we seem to be short on miracles in the foster child area.

I read once about Boys Town, now called Boys and Girls Town. They have nice little cottages, each with a few kids and a mother and father figure and everyone is happy. Why can't there be more places like that?

I dreamed last night that Joanne and I had a special calling to report how bad and sad foster homes can be. I don't know how we are going to go about getting that done. I just know we have to do it!

Tuesday, November 15

It is amazing how life sometimes places one where they should be.

Our foster home had a fire in the kitchen and family room, and while no one was hurt, all the kids had to be shuffled to other places. Joanne and I feel beyond lucky that we were allowed to stay together. But now we feel totally required to let someone in power know about what is happening to maybe millions of help-less, mistreated kids. It's time adults stopped closing their minds and hearts! The question is how can two dumb kids like Joanne and I do anything?

Hmmmm . . . I can see Sister Mary standing before me with her hands folded tightly together, saying, "Where there is a will, there is a way," and "The only difference between can and can't is *T*, which stands for try!"

Joanne and I are so blessed to be in this lovely foster home, in this lovely town, with its lovely school! It's just a little over a year old, and the library is filled with wonderful up-to-date books! The teacher in my homeroom, Miss Maeberry, is a real lady. I love every-thing about her already and hope I can stay here till it's time for me to go to college. I've got to go to college somehow! I've really got to find a way!

Bob and Marie are our house parents. They are a young married couple and are comfortable with us calling them by their first names. They have rules in the house that are fair and considerate. They treat us with respect and the five kids who were here before us all seem to be well-bred kids instead of street trash. Not that I have anything against throw-away street trash. l have been there, done that! And it is the worst humiliation and degradation that a human being can endure.

Just one kid here, Doug, seems out of place, but everybody is trying to help him, love him, and care for him, with Bob and Marie's help! Only once since we've been here has Doug gotten out of control. Then instead of screaming and swearing and beating on things, like many foster parents do, Bob gently took Doug into his office and lovingly and understandingly talked to him for about an hour while the rest of us did our homework.

When Doug came back he was subdued and he apologized to all of us. Then Marie sat with him and helped him with his math.

This foster home is like a dream come true. All of us obviously have been taken from our parents, for one reason or another, but here we feel safe.

Safe is a wonderful feeling!

Joanne and I, as well as all the others, I'm sure, feel privileged to live here!

Bob and Marie Goster are the kind of parents every kid in the world would love to have! They are just living here until the Williamses come in. We hope that won't be for a long, long time.

Thursday, November 17

Last night each one of us foster kids told something about ourselves, not the horrible things that we're all pretending did not happen! Most of us found something funny to say, except Joanne, who told us all how she'd never known what "love" really was until she met me, then we all scrambled together on the floor and hugged like we'd all be here together, forever!

Most of the kids had come from very bad backgrounds, which made me too embarrassed to ever even mention the huge estate I came from with a swimming pool and tennis court and practically everything else that money can buy.

I miss Mama so much I can't allow myself to even think about her. I hurt to my bones when I even wonder about how she is and where she is. Once I dreamed Daddy had just dumped her out on the side of the road like he did me and she had to do anything she could to take care of her drug habit. I was sick for a couple of days after that. Marie thought I had the flu, but no physical thing could be as horrifically painful as a mental thing. I wish I could talk to Marie about all the lies I've been living, but I can't. Maybe someday, though . . . I hope! I hope! I hope!

Friday, December 2

I've been so busy and happy for the past few weeks that I haven't taken time to write. Actually I feel so safe and secure and loved here that I can even think about Mark's party without being in anguish. Maybe someday he and I will meet again. That could be possible now that I'm beginning to find myself. Imagine crumpled throw-away, street kid, me . . . finding me!

Monday, December 12

Marie woke up during the night with nausea. Bob came into my room and asked if I'd come help him take care of her. He had an appointment with the university president at eight thirty A.M., and Marie, sick as she was, insisted that he go. It was a three-hour drive to the university, so time was of the essence. Marie and I both assured him that if her vomiting didn't stop soon I would call their doctor.

It really made me feel good when they both said I was the most mature youngster they had had in their home and they both trusted me implicitly. Bob had his cell phone with him, and I promised I would call him for the very smallest thing.

Marie stopped throwing up shortly after Bob left, but I still stayed home from school. I feel so honored to answer the phone and give information to the caller; actually Marie tells me what to do and say, but

I still feel important! More important than I have felt in . . . forever! At last I have a life! Marie says, if I want to, I can help her with some of the books and charts and things. Do I want to? Wow! I wish there was a Catholic church close so I could go light some candles.

Saturday, December 17

I'm doing lots of things to help Marie. She pays me but she knows she doesn't have to. I'm delighted to do anything I can to help her and Bob, or anyone else in our home! I am helping a couple of kids with their homework and Bob calls me their mentor. It makes me so proud I almost bounce off the walls. Sometimes Joanne and I whisper for what seems like hours in our bunks, about how good it is here, how lucky we are, and how someday we really are going to be somebodies!

Monday, December 19

Bob is deep into some project he is working on at the university. We're all proud of him, and I'm helping Marie with many of her books and papers and things because she's helping Bob with his research. It's fun and exciting, and there is kind of a buzz of excitement in the air. We are all working together in kind of a solidarity movement. Even Doug, who was such a nonconformist when Joanne and I moved in, has become a soft and comfortable part of the whole.

Friday, December 23

Black Friday!

Blackest day on earth!

Sad Christmas!

Today, after school, Marie and Bob called us all together and we sat on the floor in the living room in a circle, holding hands.

We could tell by the look on Marie and Bob's faces that something really bad had happened and I guess the others, like me, wondered what in the world it could be. Did Marie have cancer? Had Bob been in an accident and killed someone? Was he going to jail? Would the police be at our door in a few minutes to take him away? Were Bob and Marie getting a divorce? Other thoughts, more horrific than that, were trying to infiltrate into my brain. Then I noticed Bob sitting next to Joanne. Tears were running down his face as he pulled her hand up to his mouth and said, in a croaky wet whisper, "I love you, little Joanne." He looked around the room and told the rest of us how we would, for the rest of his life, be part of his heart.

Doug gasped, "Are you going to die?"

Marie seemed stronger than Bob at that point and she told us that Bob had been chosen to be a professor at the university. She would have to go with him. It was something he had looked forward to his whole life but he didn't have any idea that he would be given that distinguished honor so soon. Marie went on to tell us how he had filled every requirement without a single flaw, two years before, but he had been considered too young.

Then, on Thursday, Professor Maynard had been killed in an automobile accident, and Bob was asked to take his place after going through eight hours of careful enquiries. As of now it would be a temporary position and maybe . . . but we all knew it wouldn't be temporary . . . we have lost him forever. Tears were running down our faces and down the front of our clothes like water spouts. Each of us throw-aways knew that he would be the closest thing to a real father we would probably ever have.

Saturday, January 7

The next week passed in a flash. Bob and Marie drove off into the sunset, leaving us alone in the cold, dark house. They had taken all the sunshine and joy with them and we were left again with strangers: Mr. and Mrs. Williams. They said we could call them Mom and Dad if we wanted to later on, when we knew them better. But they aren't our mom or dad, they are strangers, cold, stony, old, yucky, uncaring strangers. Marie had promised us we would like them . . . but none of us want to like them. We want Bob and Marie back.

Tuesday, February 14

Five weeks have passed and there still is no joy or sunshine in our lives. We miss Marie and Bob so much that we are all like shadows of the people we once were.

It is really scary to know that I have lost myself again. I wonder if the other kids feel as thoroughly depleted and bereaved as I do.

I give Joanne all the attention and love I can, but it's hard to give something you don't have anymore!

It's terrifying and dreadful to feel as alone and empty as I think we all feel.

Doug is thinking of running away and becoming a street kid again. Teddy and Jim are talking about going with him.

Joanne and I are trying to get them to stay for a little while and give Mr. and Mrs. Williams a chance. I think they are really trying, but they seem so dull and empty after Bob and Marie, that it really is hard to go by their sissy baby rules and silly, dumb regulations. We feel like robots devoid of any self-management or thinking.

We're told when to go to bed, when to wake up, when to make our beds, when to study, when to eat, when to clean up, etc.

With Bob and Marie Goster, we were free and easy spirits, filled with enthusiasm and lively animation. We were encouraged to try new things, improve, grow, relish finding higher planes. In some ways the Gosters were a lot like the nuns. In other ways, very different, but both the nuns and the Gosters encouraged kids to look for the exciting and educational dreams life offered, to always soar upward toward our glorious futures. Mr. and Mrs. Williams make us feel like slices of stale bread waiting for ourselves to mold away into nothingness.

Thursday, February 16

Today Miss McNamarra asked me to stay after school for a few minutes. I said I would but I'm not looking forward to Mrs. Williams handing down extra chores for coming home late. Nor am I looking forward to walking . . . maybe running . . . the three miles home if I miss my bus. That sounds mean and self-centered and childish! Actually, Mrs. Williams isn't mean. I think maybe we foster kids are taking our pain out on her and her husband just because we miss Bob and Marie Goster so much!

I'm so ashamed! We all should sit down with the Williamses and apologize for being so self-centered; then maybe we can have a great relationship with them, too.

By the time school was out I'd chewed my fingernails on my right hand down to the skin, in fact on my pinky finger a little blood was oozing through some cracked skin. Miss McNamarra saw it and immediately got me a Band-aid. Then she told me she had been deeply worried about me for the past few weeks since the Gosters left, and she wondered if there was something she could do to help.

She put her arm around me and I felt like summer and sunshine and lilacs and love had come back into my life. Next to Marie and Bob, I loved Miss McNamarra most of all. She treated me like I was "almost a somebody" and trusted me to prepare and pass papers and run errands for her. She also had me help kids who were having trouble with their schoolwork.

When she told me I was her favorite student, I fell completely apart. I hadn't had anyone tell me I was their favorite anything in so long that I could hardly believe it.

Tears fell and I blew my nose and sniffed and gagged

and choked and started chewing on the fingernails again.

Miss McNamarra put my hands in hers and told me she was going to drive me home. On the way we could talk about what was hurting me inside. She said she could feel my pain. It seemed so dark and dangerous that she knew I needed help and felt that she, maybe, was the one who could find help for me.

My heart started cautiously singing, as she parked under a big shade tree by Miller's Stream. "Feel like talking?" she asked quietly.

I didn't think I wanted to, or dared to, but before I knew it I was telling Miss McNamarra about Daddy beating Mama. I didn't want to tell her but the words sloshed out and her tears joined mine as I went through the rest of my sordid life. Especially the Hollywood Hades, and the Los Angeles Skid Row nightmare. Those ever-lasting experiences will, every minute of every day for the rest of my life, be with me, part of me, making me, in all ways, unworthy to ever even touch another person. They were so dreadful, filthy, evil, diabolic and satanic, that I will never feel clean again for the rest of my life.

Miss McNamarra hugged me so tightly I thought something would break, but it felt good too and maybe she was squashing some of the ugliness and filth out! At least I hoped so!

Suddenly we were both crying like broken faucets. Miss McNamarra's voice was so waterlogged that I could hardly understand her. She was trying to tell me that, sad and dehumanizing as it was, there were thousands, probably millions of innocent children who were being so abominably and detestably used.

I felt like she had been one of us! She didn't say so in words, but the way she shivered and the way her voice broke without her actually mentioning a single detail almost assured me she was.

On the rest of the ride to the Williamses, Miss McNamarra told me that it was good to vent and she promised that she would find some help for me. When she said that, I broke down again and told her how I'd said I was fourteen, when I first went to the Salvation Army, because I thought if they knew I had just turned sixteen, they might think I was old enough to be on the streets by myself. Then I told her how I'd hated, detested, abhorred myself for being such a stupid liar.

She giggled a little at that and told me that she had, right away, known that I was bright . . . no, brilliant, and that she had admired me, I can't even remember all the wondrous things she poured out upon me. Then she looked me straight in the eyes and said that God could forgive me for the lie . . . but for those who had abused me . . . she shook her head mournfully.

We stopped to get ice cream before Miss McNamarra took me to the Williamses. She said we were both so messed up and tear-streaked that we'd scare all the kids in the house if we didn't get straightened out before we got there.

Mrs. Williams was nice as pie to Miss McNamarra. She even thanked her for letting me be her aide. She also told Miss McNamarra how much she loved us kids and how they hoped to soon be using the rules Bob and Marie used. Does she really mean that?

Friday, February 17

Today Miss McNamarra and I went for a little walk during lunch period. She told me about the good in the Williamses. She said they worked in a different kind of way than the Gosters, but in a way that made them one of the most respected foster homes in the group.

"Yeah, yeah," I said. "Robots usually make good slaves."

Miss McNamarra laughed and said that while I might not like the strictness I would, later on in my life, respect the discipline, which most kids in foster care desperately needed.

Before I could say, "Not me," she said it for me and we giggled like Jennifer and I used to! It made me feel better than I had in a long time.

Friday, March 3

Two weeks have passed and I am almost eighteen, pretending to be almost fifteen. I'm small-boned and thin so no one has called me on it but . . . I hate lying . . . I hate pretending . . . I hate having Miss McNamarra knowing that I'm every minute of every day living a lie. I hate being in the ninth grade, when I should be in the eleventh grade. I hate having to be doing material two grades below where I should be. I hate everything! Nobody relates to me anymore, nor I to them!

Miss McNamarra had promised me, well . . . maybe not promised me . . . but told me that she was almost sure she could find a place where I would belong. I guess she forgot about it . . . and me!

All I can do is cry and cry and cry . . . and want to die! Die! Die!

Why not? What is left for me? My life is no life! My dad is the evilest of child molesters. My mother is a drug addict.

Jennifer, Donita, Lacy, and every other creep I've tried to help have abandoned me, even Miss "ho" McNamarra and stuck-up Joanne!

I wish I had enough money to become an addict like my mother. She was always in a soft white floating cloud of drugs or alcohol. But no! No! No! I don't!

2:30 a.m.

I just woke out of a horrendous nightmare of people hating me and picking on me, putting me back into a vile trailer family.

Life isn't worth the air it takes to breathe!

We're not even human beings here. We're zombies, with no minds of our own.

I'm getting out of here!

Tomorrow night I'm going to sneak out and go on the streets. Anything is better than this!

I know Jackie Cramer is a pusher at school and on the street. I'll hook up with him. He's cute and he's smart and his dad is a doctor at the hospital. That will make me a somebody, a bad somebody . . . but that's better than being a nobody nothing!

I know I'll have to "give something" to "get something." But after a while I'll have my own little ring, and who cares what I do with my hopeless, sordid, worthless life? What life?

Wednesday, March 8

I've been looking for Jackie Cramer for two days but I can't find him. Everything in the universe is against me.

Miss McNamarra has been trying to cozy up to me, but anything she's got I don't want! She's hurt me too much in the past, by making me feel . . . maybe . . .

then dropping me . . . like I was about as important as dog poo.

I still do her idiotic little passing out junk and picking up stuff and running errands to the supply office, etc. But not for much longer!

Friday, March 10

Today Miss McNamarra asked me to come back to her room after my last class. That filled me with so much anger and pain and hate, and everything else bad, that by the time I got to her room I was about to detonate.

She was kind of laughing and crying at the same time. That made me want to reach out and hit her, until she handed me a letter from a Mrs. Mary Matthews, who lived in Westwood, really close to UCLA. She was a professor at UCLA and she wanted to meet me! Me? Why?

Miss McNamarra is going to take me there tomorrow but she doesn't want to give me a lot of details. It's almost like it's a birthday secret or something.

I must not get my hopes up too high, though. Please, please God, let it be something at least a little bit nice.

I am so regretful and feel wretched about my feelings for Miss McNamarra the last few days. How could I ever have thought such vile, evil things about her? Probably because I was trying to dump my insecurities and aloneness and excruciating torment off myself and onto her.

Saturday, March 11

1:33 a.m.

I woke up like someone had hit me on the head with a hammer. What if Mrs. Williams wouldn't let me go spend the day with Miss McNamarra and Mrs. Mary Matthews?

Her name put a warm, protective glow around my body. I had to meet her!

Would she be like dear, sweet, Sister Mary at the Catholic girls' school? My whole body pulsed with the warm, protective love that had been showered upon us there.

4:20 a.m.

For the past few hours, I've been kneeling beside my bed, asking for forgiveness regarding the terrible things I have been thinking for a pretty long time now. I am so ashamed! Can I ever be forgiven?

5:15 a.m.

I woke up still kneeling at the side of my bed . . . but . . . I wasn't feeling angry or hateful or hurtful to anyone, or anything, in God's whole universe. Love and appreciation seemed to be wrapping me gently toward them. I wanted it to be a forever and ever and ever feeling!

6:00 a.m.

Mrs. Williams woke me up early so that I could get my Saturday chores done before Miss McNamarra picked me up at 7:30 A.M. My heart was beating like a drum in a parade. Mrs. Williams hadn't even mentioned why I was going. Maybe she really didn't care.

Saturday night

I can't believe I'm not dreaming! Miss McNamarra picked me up and we had breakfast at Uncle John's Pancake House. We laughed and teased, and I begged for some little hint about what was going to happen, but Miss McNamarra just pretended she was zipping up her mouth and we went on to something else nice. It was a beautiful day! Even the smog seemed beautiful!

When we drove down Wilshire Boulevard, just a dozen or so blocks south of my old house, I cried a few tears. Miss McNamarra told me that was all right and in a few minutes I was again bubbling inside.

When Mary Matthews met us at her door I almost

fell down. She looked so much like I had hoped she would look. And when she took both of my dry dishpan hands and held them in her soft fragrant ones, I wanted to pull away I was so embarrassed.

We went out into her lovely little garden behind her lovely little house and talked for a long time about UCLA, and then she told me her life story: how her mother and father had been killed in an automobile accident when she was eight and how she had been raised by her father's mother in Venice. They were very poor and had lived in a dangerous neighborhood. Never before she was fourteen had she been allowed to go out after it got dark.

After her grandma Zelkaleke, died she was placed in a group home for girls, where she was considered the house nerd because books were her only friends. She was picked on constantly, and what little confidence she ever had soon faded away.

When she was seventeen, she met Robert Lynn Matthews in a history class, and when she was eighteen and a half, she married him. They were enchanted by books and history and music and every other educational thing. Eventually they both became happy, excited Ph.D.s. But . . . they were never been able to have children.

About a year ago Robert died of heart failure. Mary felt her life had gone with him until she met Miss

McNamarra who said Mary needed *me* as much as I needed *her* and that we were so much alike in our desire to help others that we would be exactly like mother and daughter.

I broke down in tears when I heard that, and when Mary asked me if I would like to be her daughter, my heart leaped around in my breast like a wild thing.

I'll still be living with Mr. and Mrs. Williams for the next few weeks, until all the papers are signed and stuff. Until then I will try to undo some of the selfish, mean thoughts I've had about the Williamses, especially Mrs. Williams! I'm sorry to the deepest part of me that I allowed myself to think she was like an army major, cracking the whip at us at every chance. That isn't how it was at all. She was just trying to help us, teach us discipline and respect for things and people. Maybe she was a little extreme, but she meant well, and our house is the highest-rated house in the group. I am so, so, so sorry I was so negative!

Sacred Sunday, April 9

I am living with my dear mother Mary now, and my cup runneth over. Mom took me to see Sister Mary at my old Catholic school, and my cup ran over again. I am blessed!

Mom tutors me every night so I can catch up and

climb higher on my educational mountain. Soon I'll be going back into the class I belong in. I didn't realize until now how humiliating and self-confidence-depleting it was being with kids almost three years younger than I!

Thank you God. Thank you Jesus. Thank you Mother Mary of Jesus! I promise I will never again in my life let any of you down. . . . Well, I'll try my best not to. And I am going to live the rest of my life helping others: teaching or counseling or working with "throw-away kids" who hopefully will wind up as lucky and blessed as I am.

I HAVE FOUND MYSELF!
I AM
KATHRYN MATTHEWS
• DAUGHTER OF ROBERT LYNN AND
MARY MATTHEWS.

I'm hoping someday Mom will help me find Lacy and Donita. Also I want to have a long, long talk with Sister Mary and ask her if God can forgive me and make me completely clean and worthy again. I feel guilty not wanting to talk to a priest . . . but since the Daddy thing . . . no way! At least not for now!

Wednesday, April 12

Mom is on a number of important boards and she just called and said that when she talked about how many throw-away kids there were in the system, including the foster homes, the other members were dumbfounded. All of them, without exception, wanted to do some work in that area. I'm sure Miss McNamarra told Mom much more than I would have liked . . . but maybe not . . . because she certainly couldn't have gotten much out of me.

My heart is beating so fast it's almost trying to jump out of my body. Could it possibly be that every throw-away kid in the system could be as lucky as I?

Tears are thundering down my face because I know *that* is not possible. But I can pray for it!

Dearest Mom knows some people in high political offices, and she and I are going to work together regarding throw-away kids in foster homes. I can't believe that I am somebody who can make a difference! But I am! I am somebody! For eternity!

Statistics

Not all foster homes are bad, but enough of them are that they should be carefully monitored.

Half a million children live in foster homes in the United States.

Thousands of children around the world are sold as sex slaves.

Source

Federal Bureau of Investigation, National Crime Information Center.

The FBI estimates that 85–90% of missing persons are juveniles. Thus, children are involved in approximately 750,000 cases (2,100 per day).

"Endangered"—120.726 cases.

Throw-aways

Broad Scope Throw-aways: 127,100 children
- the child was told to leave the household
- the child was away from home and a parent/

guardian refused to allow the child back

- the child ran away but the parent/guardian made no effort to recover the child or did not care whether or not the child returned
- the child was abandoned or deserted

Nonfamily Abductions

Children aged four to eleven experienced most of the attempts. Most involved attempts to lure children into cars rather than attempts to take or detain. Almost half of the victims were children age twelve and older. Seventy-four percent were girls. Sixty-two percent of the perpetrators were strangers and nineteen percent were acquaintances. Most were removed from the street (fifty-two percent) and taken to a vehicle. Force was used against eighty-seven percent of the victims; it involved a weapon in seventy-five percent of the cases. Ransom was requested in eight percent of the cases.

HOW MANY CHILDREN ARE SEXUALLY APPROACHED AND/OR SOLICITED ONLINE?

According to highlights of the Youth Internet Safety Survey conducted by the U.S. Department of Justice "one in five children (ages ten to seventeen) receive unwanted sexual solicitations online." So be careful!

Questions, Answers, and Crisis Lines

Once while talking to a large group of young people about the book I was working on, I sensed trepidation in some of them. It made shivers go up and down my spine, and I gently suggested that they might want to write to me regarding situations they know about or predicaments that have come their way. I was totally amazed, totally depressed, and totally angered by the number of heartbroken letters I received! How can kids at any age be treated so shamefully? Twenty young people wrote about being beaten *often!*

Here are some examples of their letters:

No name (a boy): *My mom and dad were having marital problems; she thought he had a girlfriend. Their quarreling and screaming got me crazy and I started hanging out at the mall. There at a "car game" I met Jeff. He was a lot older than me but he loved cars and told me he'd take me for a drive in his red* convertible. A couple of days later he let me drive even though I'm only fifteen. Jeff was my idol! I wanted to be just like him. 1. Slowly we went from a few raunchy flicks while drinking a little beer and smoking a little weed. 2. Then on to porno and harder drugs. 3. He gave me a drug and raped me. 4. I guess that was my dumb fault, but now I've got some sores and I'm afraid to go to the doctor. I wish I knew what to do.

NO NAME: *I am a schoolteacher who was raped by my two teenage cousins when I was little. I now am married and have three children but the "fear factor" in my life has never let up. Please, please help me to dump my thirty-year horror movie! It still, at odd times, comes back in front of my eyes like it was happening again. How could my parents not have known? What would they have done if I had told them? Did my cousins do it to other little girls? I wish I knew someone I dared talk to. I think, even writing this to you, a stranger, has lifted up the weight a little.*

If you have been abused in any way, find someone to talk to: a parent, a school counselor, or a clergy person.

Telephone information! Ask them to get you a number for a child abuse hotline.

Remember that if you have been abused by a father, grandfather, mother, or anyone else, you are most likely not the only person they have abused!

Crisis Lines

You can call any crisis line in your local telephone book, or you can call any of the following free numbers:

- Sexual Assault Crisis Line (1-800-643-6250)
- Boys Town (which now includes girls) (1-800-448-3000)
- Hope Line (1-800-656-4673)
- National Youth Crisis Hotline (1-800-448-4663)